Editing by Maggie Sokolik

Cover design by D.J. Rogers, Book Branders

ISBN: 978-1-93875-789-1

72721

---

This is a work of fiction.

The word "Indian" is sometimes used to refer to Native Americans, in recognition that this term is in use in the Native American community.

# TREASURE SEEKERS

## TRANSYLVANIAN TRILOGY #3

### ROBERTA SERET

WAYZGOOSE PRESS

# IN APPRECIATION

No book is written alone.

Words and thoughts come alive on the page only after they are shared with those the author esteems. I have been fortunate to have family and friends who have believed in me. For without them, my literary world could not have taken shape.

My deepest appreciation goes to each one of you:

Maggie Sokolik, Senior Editor, Fiction, Wayzgoose Press; Dorothy Zemach, Publisher, Wayzgoose Press; Marcia Rockwood, my editor; DJ Rogers, Book Branders for book covers; Marissa Eigenbrood and her Team at Smith Publicity; Natalia Donofrio, my web designer; Mridula Agarwal, my right hand and tech guru;

My friends of many years: Judith Vogel, Leslie and Norman Leben, Lydia Eviatar, Judith Auslander, Candida Iodice, Raffaella Depero, Nancy Cushing-Jones, Will Nix, Elise Strauss, Nina Saglimbeni, Andreea Mihut, Ioana and Eugen Mihut, Sandra Segal, Sylvia and Ira Seret.

My colleagues at the United Nations and all the teachers I admire: Kyle Ridley.

Greenwich Pen Women and Anita Keire, Ginger Heller, and Deb Weir.

My sons: Greg and Cliff; my daughters-in-law: Hally and Arielle: my grandchildren: Annabel, Sam, Jack, and Tucker.

And my husband, Michel, who always at my side, has shared his story and our journey. Without his *joie de vivre*, his optimism, his strength, these books would not have come to be.

Thank you all, Roberta

**For Michel**

*If I were to be asked what I feel is the truest accomplishment of my career,
I would answer to write Transylvanian Trilogy.
And yet, my books could not have been written if I had not lived my life
to its fullest, with you.*

# INTRODUCTION

Dear Reader,

I invite you to go on a voyage with me to Transylvania where my imagination has borrowed political intrigues to create a different view of Literature. Facts fuse with fiction in *Transylvanian Trilogy.*

*Gift of Diamonds, Love Odyssey,* and *Treasure Seekers,* each book of the trilogy, can be read independently or interchanged, depending on reader's choice. The main characters are Mica, Anca, Cristina, and Marina, four friends since their teenaged days in Transylvania, who appear and reappear in each book. They were known in their little town as best friends, the Four Musketeers, *Poets of their Lives.*

*Gift of Diamonds* is Mica's story and her escape with rare colored diamonds as Communism in Romania explodes under dictator, Ceausescu.

*Love Odyssey* is Anca's quest as she escapes alone while pregnant from those who have targeted her.

Marina and Cristina take center stage in *Treasure Seekers* when they are successful women living in New York City and Paris, and vacation together to beautiful Turkey to fall, unexpectedly, into a web of terrorists.

The stories flow together amidst Romania's politics. I have used the historical settings as a novelist would–to enhance the fictional storyline. Yet, I must confess, I have sometimes been tempted to make the history a little more exciting with touches of imagination. Accordingly, I've taken liberties under the guise of "poetic license" with time and place to recreate a literary fresco of Romania's second half of the 20<sup>th</sup> century. The history is the "backdrop curtain" of the novels, not center stage.

I have used Romania's dictatorial regimes to create an atmosphere of deceit that poisoned all Romanians during the Fascist and Communist years. One form of totalitarian government led to another. These were times of secret police, informers, fear, lies, double-crossing, dehumanization, shredding of documents, the destruction of the human soul. What we know today about these times is still masked with inconsistencies and ambiguities to cover up the truth.

Yet, the world I offer you is of fiction, and I use four female characters as dramatic voices. Each woman of the trilogy takes center stage to create her own life as she journeys through political events to survive. Each one becomes involved with history and forges forward in an existentialist need to direct her own destiny. But sometimes, the four friends find challenges that are stronger than their willpower. Those are the times when the fictional protagonists merge and interact with factual events. It is then that their courage evokes exciting narratives—fiction that could not exist without truth.

I hope you enjoy this colorful kaleidoscope of fact with fiction, truth with crimes, history and art, strife with love. For it is from my heart that I offer you these stories from Transylvania.

Roberta Seret, Ph.D.

# 1

*New York City*
*January 8, 2017*

RUBBING sleep from her dark eyes, Marina Johannes took the circular steps from the second floor of her bedroom suite to the first floor of her Fifth Avenue duplex penthouse. She was already calculating her day, considering how much time she needed with her team of researchers at the Soho lab. She estimated that it would take at least three hours to review which herbs and plants they could consider for the new, organic line. They were searching for a long-lasting, natural property that would hydrate the skin during sultry weather. After that, she would need two hours uptown at her Madison Avenue and 51$^{st}$ Street showroom to review the spring mail-order brochure with the art department.

Marina was New York's leading cosmetologist, having made her reputation on her expertise for making women's skin more beautiful.

She put the lights on in the kitchen and looked out onto the terrace to Central Park, which was a vision of snow. It reminded her of mornings in Romania when she was a girl, and the trees in Transylvania were covered in white frost. Her mother would prepare for her tea with honey and toast, thick with rose petal jam. Marina felt the same way now—happy, for she was already planning her trip in March to see her friends, Mica, Anca, and Cristina, in Paris for Cristina's fashion show.

Marina opened her computer on the marble counter to check the day's news, and then switched on the espresso machine. She waited a minute until the beans ground automatically and a shot of espresso flowed into her cup.

She sipped her coffee while she scanned the news and then stopped, startled, as she read the headline:

### RAFSANJANI, IRAN'S MOST POWERFUL MAN, IS DEAD

She read on:

Akbar Hashemi Rafsanjani, one of the founding fathers of the Islamic Republic of Iran, died today in Tehran, January 8th, 2017, at the age of eighty-three. He was considered by many to be the richest man in Iran. He was president of his country from 1989-1997.

1989. It had been Christmas season in Romania. There were no holiday dinners that year, no good tidings, not even heat. It was a time of revolution, bloody uprisings and people dying for freedom. Ceausescu had been executed on Christmas day, his death, a gift to all Romanians. Yet, there was a mystery about the days before his execution. Why had he traveled to Tehran with dozens of trunks when there was a revolution going on in Romania? It was said that Ceausescu had deposited $1 billion dollars-worth of gold in Rafsanjani's new private bank.

Marina remembered that after Ceausescu's death, the revolutionaries took inventory of the dictator's wealth–his palaces, his art collection, his diamonds, even his hunting lodge walled with gold coins and bathrooms with 14-karat gold toilet seats. She wondered what had happened to Ceausescu's gold in Iran. The Romanian government was never able to find it. No one from his family had ever claimed it. Had it remained in Tehran with the president?

Yet Rafsanjani did not have enough time to spend Ceausescu's billion dollars worth of gold. Under his administration, Iran had been sanctioned because of terrorism and its uranium enrichment programs. Iran's economy was blocked. How could he get gold out of the country? Especially since, after his presidency, he was suspected by his political enemies of being such a rich businessman.

She wondered who could have helped Rafsanjani with his gold from Ceausescu's corrupt deals and terrorist partnerships with Gaddafi, Arafat, Ali Bhutto, and North Korea's Kim Jung Il. A billion dollars of gold from Romania, such a poor country, while the people lived for twenty-four years under a ruthless dictatorship with little food, little heat, little light, no rights, no freedom, no life. Marina wished she knew what had happened to that gold, deposited in Tehran.

No one had found the treasure in all these years. Yet questions surrounding its fate lingered in Marina's thoughts, as they did in the thoughts of many alongside her, trying to find their way out of the legacy of deprivation the dictator had left them.

Marina made herself another cup of espresso and continued:

**Iran and Turkey, Partners in Gold**

Speculation about gold laundering between Iran and Turkey has led American prosecutors to the world's richest gold smuggler, Recep Sharatt, who was arrested last year in Miami on

March 19, 2016. He had been on record for past crimes committed in the States.

Sharatt is thirty-three years old, has quadruple citizenship from Iran, Turkey, Azerbaijan, and Macedonia, and has amassed a fortune. He was charged with being the one who had laundered the gold for Iran and Turkey. His holdings include twenty mansions, nine yachts, two private helicopters, a jet plane, a stable of Arabian horses, sports cars, Impressionist paintings, and a gold-plated pistol.

There was a photo of Sharatt, looking calm and confident, answering questions from journalists, as he was being transferred from Miami to a Manhattan prison.

The reporters wanted to learn more about him. Why had he come to the United States when he knew he'd be arrested? They called him an enigma; someone not to be trusted.

### From the U.S. Department of Justice

### Office of Public Affairs

**FOR IMMEDIATE RELEASE**

An indictment was unsealed in the Southern District of New York against Recep Sharatt, a resident of Turkey and citizen of Turkey and other countries, for engaging in hundreds of millions of dollars-worth of transactions on behalf of the government of Iran and Iranian entities, which were barred by U.S. sanctions. He is accused of laundering the proceeds of illegal transactions and defrauding eight financial institutions that have their headquarters in New York City. Sharatt was arrested on March 19, 2016, in Miami's international airport, and then transferred to a Manhattan prison on March 28, 2016.

Recep Sharatt is charged with conspiracies to defraud the United States, to violate international embargo laws, to commit bank fraud, and to commit money laundering. His conspiracy to defraud the United States carries a maximum sentence of fifty-five years in prison. Any sentencing of the defendant will be determined by the judge of the case.

The charges contained in this indictment are merely accusations, and the defendant is presumed innocent unless and until proven guilty.

Marina put down the *Times*, took an apple from the counter, peeled it, and returned her attention to the map featured in the article. She saw the bold letters: ROMANIA. She remembered Ceausescu's trial, a trial that had been aired on TV on Christmas day, just hours before he and his wife had been executed. The judge of the case had told Ceausescu, "You would have been better off to have stayed in Tehran with your gold."

Ceausescu went to Tehran on December 18, 1989, and stayed two days. He returned to Bucharest with a group of Iranian Revolutionary Guards to protect him, compliments of president Rafsanjani. It was the peak of Romania's bloody Revolution.

Marina's thoughts went to Sharatt, the Iranian and Turkish citizen who was arrested in the United States. What was he doing in Miami?

Then her cell phone rang and interrupted her thoughts. It was her assistant, Janet, saying she'd be twenty minutes late for their meeting—New York traffic. Marina told her not to rush, and returned to finish the article:

Sharatt was detained at Miami's airport as he went through Customs. He entered the States with his wife, Deniz Akar, Turkey's famous rock singer and music composer for cinema. Traveling with them was their five-year-old daughter.

They were on their way to visit Disney World. But he was taken into custody because of a criminal record issued by the District Attorney's Office of the Southern district of New York dating from 2013. Sharatt was subsequently flown to New York City, booked and imprisoned for conspiring to evade international sanctions.

In 2013, he was accused by the District Attorney's Office of the Southern district of New York *in absentia,* as an accomplice to eight international banks that have headquarters in Manhattan and are under investigation for facilitating the laundering of money for Iran. Sharatt was their conduit to the scheme. For this reason, he was taken from Miami to be booked and incarcerated in Manhattan.

His wife and daughter were immediately released in Miami and allowed to return to Istanbul. Sharatt's trial date is set for November 2017; that is, if there is no interference. Judge Robert Friedman, who is presiding over the case, has detained Sharatt in Manhattan's Correction Center without bail because of his *political connections.*

The Attorney General's office of Manhattan explained why there would be no bail: "There are powerful political leaders involved in this case. Sharatt has a personal contact with the president of Turkey, Riza Tarik Ozogant, whose administration is directly involved in this case.

Ozogant has already spoken several times about Sharatt's

detention to President Hommett who has contacted Attorney
General Larissa Linde to discuss extradition for Sharatt. President Ozogant would do anything to get him back to Turkey.
The court doesn't trust that if Sharatt goes free on bail, that
he'd remain in the States. There are also his relations with Iran.

Marina studied the map. She hoped there'd be more news in
the coming days, news about Turkey and Iran... and the final days
of Romania's dictator with all that gold.

# 2

*Le Jardin du Luxembourg, Paris*
*March 9, 2017*

"AVANCEZ! START NOW," came the clear orders from Cristina Patrisse, Paris's leading fashion designer. "*Passez*," she told each of the twelve models as they marched one by one into Le Jardin du Luxembourg. It was the first fashion show in Paris that had ever been held outdoors in the city's famous garden.

Cristina pressed the button for Ravel's *Bolero* suite, and the sounds of horns announced each model's appearance. It was springtime in Paris, and Cristina was introducing her new collection of fashionable headwear. Each was adorned with a jewel using a design copied from Salvador Dali, and each of the twelve models wore a headpiece representing a month of the year, with a jewel clipped to the front. Cristina's assistant handed the journalists a corresponding photo of Dali's original jewel as each model circled the pond.

Marina sat in the middle of Mica and Anca, while applauding Cristina's creativity in matching the model's color of hat with color of dress and color of jewel. Laughing like children, the friends delighted at each month's design: December, January, and February were made in Russian Cossack-style hats from mink, fox, and chinchilla. March, April, and May were designed from feathers of blue jay, red cardinal, and yellow finch. June, July, and August had sweeping brims of orange and purple straw. September, October, and November were made from silks in autumn colors.

Beauty and art combined with the exotic to stamp Cristina's mark on Paris's fashion world.

A cocktail reception followed, held outdoors adjacent to the Musée du Luxembourg, the museum in the park. Cristina had coordinated every detail and arranged the buffet table with pink and red tulips next to red and pink azalea bushes. She stood at the head of the table and greeted each guest. When her three friends approached from the congratulatory line, she whispered to them, "Thank God it didn't rain. I've been checking the weather report every five minutes."

Marina didn't dare ask Cristina about alternative plans. She just smiled as she kissed her friend cheek-to-cheek.

"We should celebrate you," Anca said, toasting Cristina with a glass of champagne.

"I'll accept that," the designer agreed. "Dinner tonight, the four of us, without our men. In any event, if I'm correct, André is in New York seeing patients." She addressed her friend Mica. "Right? And Petre is with Eugen." She turned to Anca to see if she knew that both their husbands were together and where they were. Anca looked concerned, and Cristina tried to console her with a quick response. "I'm sure wherever they are, they have back-up protection."

Anca took out her cellphone to show Cristina why she was worried. "A news flash about a Turkish gold smuggler who was arrested in New York and his accomplices who were politicians.

The D.A.'s office in Manhattan is opening up the case again. I wonder if Petre and Eugen are involved in this? Sounds like something that fits their expertise. Petre stayed in New York instead of joining me in Paris. I wondered why. Do you think Eugen is with him in New York?" she asked. "Or do you think they went to another hotspot together?"

"Unfortunately, Eugen never tells me the details of his work. He's very secretive," Cristina commented. "At breakfast, he tells me if he's here in Paris for the day or if he's traveling. Where he's going, he doesn't say, and I leave it at that. The next morning, he tells me where he went, and if he was working on the case with Petre, as he usually does. They have their clandestine ways, these two Transylvanian investigators."

"So, dinner tonight," Marina quickly intervened, sensing that both of her friends were concerned. "But more than that, how about a weekend vacation, all four of us? Who can get away in a few weeks to join me?"

Mica shook her head. "Can't. I have to get ready for September's opening with the troupe." Mica was the head choreographer for Martha Graham's dance group in New York. "And Luca's graduating in two months. I promised to help him move and store his furniture."

Anca shrugged her shoulders. "Sorry, ladies. I can't go either. I have new interns to train. The year's pediatric program starts July 1st."

"Well," Marina laughed, "that leaves you and me, Cristina. I've been invited to Santa Fe to sample some new facial creams made with aloe and desert herbs. And I need a change of scenery. How about joining me?"

"Delighted," Cristina replied. "Eugen will be working, and I could use a rest after staging this show. Hiking in the desert would be perfect. Maybe I'll find some exotic fabrics for a new collection."

"Yes, Santa Fe would be a practical trip, but I wish we had more time, and we could go to Istanbul," Marina commented.

"Istanbul? Why Turkey?" Cristina asked.

"I read an article in the *New York Times* about a gold smuggling crime, and I'd love to play investigator."

"If you were married to Cristina's husband or mine," Anca said, "you wouldn't want the risk. Vicariously, you'd have had enough."

"I brought the *Times* article with me, actually," Marina said, taking it out of her handbag. "It involves the country of our youth. Did anyone read it?"

"I didn't," replied Cristina. "This fashion show took all my time."

"So tell us," Mica said, teasingly, in the same tone she used when the friends, known at school as the *Four Musketeers*, bantered together as they had done since they were thirteen years old.

"A scheme involving Ceausescu's billion dollars' worth of gold that he deposited in Tehran a few days before he was executed."

"I remember his trial," Anca said. "The judge mentioned something about Ceausescu taking a fortune to a private bank in Tehran."

"That's right: a fortune in gold. But I believe it stayed there, privately, with the president, Rafsanjani. My theory is that he kept the gold a secret until a few years ago, when he reached eighty years of age, and feared he'd die with the gold stashed away. My guess is that he got it out of Iran. How, I don't know. No one knows. Maybe with the young Turkish gold smuggler, Recep Sharatt, who was imprisoned in Manhattan."

"Wow! What a theory," whistled Anca. "You have some imagination."

"First comes imagination, and then proof," Marina responded, defensively. "I'm a scientist."

Her friends laughed. "A scientist for beauty. Not crime."

"So tell us," Cristina said, coming to Marina's defense, "why would Sharatt, a citizen of Turkey, work on behalf of Iran?"

"To get rich," Marina answered. "Or maybe for another reason, something more important than money."

"That deserves to be investigated!" Anca, the doctor, said, smiling. "Did the D.A.'s Office do a psychiatric profile on him? In cases like this, they usually do that. Always interested me."

"I read that they did," Marina answered. "He seems to be extremely bright. Genius level. And that's why this case is so fascinating. I can't understand why a man like him would go to Miami for a vacation, and to Disney World!"

"Miami? Is that where he was arrested?"

"Yes. I Googled him," Marina continued, "as a way to start my research. It said on Wikipedia that he was born in Tabriz, Iran, in September 1983 to a wealthy, Iranian-Azerbaijan family. As a teenager, he began his career with several business enterprises, consisting of money transfers, currency exchanges, and gold trading. At nineteen, he left Iran by himself and moved to Istanbul, where he started his first gold brokerage/currency exchange. Made a fortune, became a Turkish citizen, and then went into shipbuilding there. All before he was twenty-one."

"And his parents? What did the article say about them?"

"His father, Hassan Sharatt, was a steel magnate and part of a team organized by President Khorasami to help work around the U.S. and U.N. sanctions due to Iran's nuclear program."

"How did Sharatt Junior get involved in Iranian gold?"

"In 2011, Iran's national petroleum company was looking for ways to transfer their money that they had made from bypassing sanctions, but legally were not allowed to accept. Billions of dollars were waiting in countries that had bought Iranian oil and did not abide by the international embargo, as was the case with China, the United Arab Emirates, Malaysia, and Malta. They were willing to pay, and the Iranian government wanted the money from these transactions." Marina was getting excited as she explained. Her cheeks were flushed, and she began talking faster and louder.

"According to some international press I've been reading, Recep became the man to circumvent the sanctions. He had experience—he had established a successful gold-brokerage-currency exchange in Istanbul, and his politically connected Iranian father had trained him well."

"Did you find anything else online that explained how Sharatt navigated the embargo sanctioned against Iran? That's no easy feat," Anca commented, taking out her cell phone and searching for more information about Recep Sharatt.

"Yes, according to the BBC and Reuters, the U.S. government believes that Sharatt used a loophole in the embargo ruling; a *legal* loophole that allows shipping food, medicine, and firefighting equipment for humanitarian purposes to a country despite sanctions. Sharatt was able to use this loophole when he began the 'Gas for Gold Scheme.'" Marina cleared her throat and added, "That's the name of the scheme—Turkey buys gas from Iran and pays Iran for it with gold."

"How did the boy wizard do this?" Cristina asked, now completely caught up in the story. "Sounds like he has a talent for deception, also. He master-minded quite a scheme."

Marina smiled; she was happy to have her friends as immersed in the case as she was. "Sharatt set up front companies where he intermingled legitimate profits with illegal money in China as well as in Azerbaijan, Russia, Turkmenistan, and the United Arab Emirates. He also wired millions to the United States where he has a shell company – an inactive company – that he used for illegal financial maneuvers. For all his business enterprises, he has his main headquarters in Trump Towers Istanbul, as well as other offices around the world, in places like Dubai and Bologna."

"I understand the strategy," Anca said, showing her friends an article on her cell phone from the Italian newspaper, *Corriere della Sera*: RECEP SHARATT BEING INVESTIGATED IN ITALY.

"The shell companies became his infrastructure," she read out loud. "Then he took advantage of a loophole that is still being analyzed."

"Yes," Marina agreed and took out a chart that she'd printed out from another *Times* article. "The journalist, a Pulitzer prize winner who's the head of the *Times* Bureau in Istanbul, has been investigating this golden loophole and found some interesting data: The gas-for-gold scheme started in 2011 and peaked in 2012 and 2013. By 2013, Turkey was exporting gold to Iran in the sum of $6.4 billion. This is compared to data that Turkey exported gold to Iran at a value of $54 million in 2011. A bit less than a $5 billion profit in two years. By 2013, Sharatt was using fifteen couriers a day to transport more than 1,000 pounds of gold daily to Iran to pay for oil and gas."

"That's a lot of gold," Anca said. "How did Turkey get so much gold?"

"That's the central question of the puzzle. I seem to recall that Turkey began the scheme with gold that Iran gave them to jump-start the operation. This was a considerable amount that set up a circular, Byzantine route to confuse officials. It moved from Iran to Turkey and then from Turkey back to Iran."

"A twisted back route to side-track everyone who thought it started in Turkey," Mica commented.

"Yes. I wish I could learn for sure where the original gold came from," Marina stated.

"Aha!" laughed Anca. "Is that why you want to travel to Turkey? Be a detective? Learn if the gold was really Ceausescu's?"

"Well, yes. To learn why we lived in poverty for twenty-four years and that monster-dictator was the richest man in Eastern Europe."

"That would certainly be worth a trip to Istanbul. But *ma chère*,"

Cristina said, "maybe another time. For now, let's go to Santa Fe. That's all the adventure I'm up for."

"Okay, Cristina. Settled for now, Santa Fe," concluded Marina, the business woman. "I'll have my secretary arrange everything. I'll buy the plane tickets—my treat to celebrate your fashion show. I'll book your ticket from Paris and mine from New York and we'll meet in Santa Fe's airport."

"Who knows?" Cristina said. "Maybe your invitation to Santa Fe isn't a coincidence at all."

"Who knows?" And Marina smiled.

# 3

THE FOUR MUSKETEERS had been friends for more than fifty years, going all the way back to grammar school in their small Transylvanian town of Spera. They considered each other to be family, and not having siblings, they were all as close as if they had been sisters.

Their friendship had solidified when Friday afternoons became a dance studio of rock 'n roll in their school gym. Mica's father supplied the students with 45-rpm records of the Beatles. No one knew where or how he had found the records in communist Romania, but find them he had, and Friday afternoons became sacred for the entire school.

The girls' friendship was more than an ordinary friendship. It was a bond that made hard times in Romania bearable. Each one realized that their friendship was a treasure never to take for granted, and they pledged from the beginning to be *One for all and all for one*; thus they became the *Four Musketeers*.

What had brought them together was a common link in their character—willpower. They recognized in one another what they respected about themselves. But their fighting spirit had as a goal not just to succeed but also to be happy.

Mica Mihailescu was at the center of her friends, but it was for Anca Rodescu that she had a special softness. Mica was always protecting Anca. During Communism, everyone was theoretically equal, but some were less deprived than others. Mica's father, Anton Mihailescu, was a professor at the engineering university and was always involved in opposition politics with many loyal contacts. He never lacked food on the table for his small family, and they were never in need of essentials.

For Anca, things were different. She had lost her parents at a young age; they had been victims of Communism. Her father, also an engineering professor and a colleague of Mica's father at the University, was arrested for opposing the dictatorship and sent to a psychiatric hospital, where torture and drugs killed him. Her mother couldn't live without him, and she too suffered from the injustices of politics. Often ill, she had difficulty facing each day, and Anca had to take care of herself. It wasn't unusual that she'd come to school without lunch. She'd never say if she had forgotten it or if there were nothing at home to take. Mica made sure that she packed twice what she needed every day, so Anca wouldn't be hungry.

Mica took the role of anchor for her friends. She had been the first of the Four Musketeers to escape Romania and had done so on her own in a daring escape. Mica's parents had been arrested for organizing an uprising against the dictator, Nicolae Ceausescu, and she realized she'd be arrested next. Knowing her father had hidden colored diamonds in their basement, she took the jewels and her bicycle and escaped in the middle of the night.

From her home near the Transylvanian-Hungarian border, she made her way to Budapest, and months later, to her uncle in New York. At a Sotheby's auction, she sold three colored diamonds for a considerable amount of money. Immediately afterwards, she dedicated herself and her money to buying her parents out of Romania. Three years after she escaped Romania, she returned to Transylvania in another daring feat to get her parents safely to New York.

And yet, despite her wealth, Mica had had to overcome many obstacles until she found her path in life. Presently, as a leading choreographer, she used classical ballet in a modern interpretation to create new programs for the stage. Her greatest pleasure was to train students to find an expression of dance that they could call their own.

Anca was the next of the Four Musketeers to escape Romania in a feat as daring as Mica's, and it was Mica who had helped her settle in New York.

Anca's story was one of great love. After medical school, Anca had specialized in infectious diseases and was sent by the communist government to the countryside to work. The clinic was in a small town in Transylvania, far away from civilization, without electricity, heat, or running water. No one would have chosen to work there, especially since there was a typhus epidemic ravaging the town.

Once there, Anca fell in love with Petre, the young doctor in charge of the clinic. Despite the hardships, they were happy. That was, until the police learned that they were secretly giving antibiotics and vaccines to non-communists and Gypsies. They feared arrest, and Petre arranged a daring escape for his pregnant wife and promised he'd soon follow. However, it took nineteen years until they were reunited when Anca returned to Romania, unknown and disguised, to save Petre, who had become Ceausescu's personal doctor and later the leader of Romania's bloody revolution of 1989.

Like Mica, Anca had dared to return to their communist country to save who she loved. Reunited in New York, Anca and Mica, together with their families, enjoyed a successful life.

Mica, from the wealth of her diamonds, next helped Cristina Patrisse and Marina Johannes when they were twenty years old by "buying" them from Ceausescu's government—they were "ethnic Germans" for sale. Mica had learned about this opportunity from her New York lawyers and made the required payments.

Cristina wanted to study fashion design in Paris, and Mica's lawyers helped her leave Romania to achieve that goal. Marina wanted to relocate to New York City, where she would have unlimited business opportunities to create something no one else had ever done before. And Mica and her lawyers helped Marina do just that—she commercialized beauty.

Marina had known at an early age what she wanted to do with her life. On Saturdays, she led her friends to the flea market outside their small town and they searched for lipsticks, nail polish and makeup. Often, there was very little available, but Marina didn't become discouraged. She found instead herbs and roots hidden under rocks in the Transylvania fields where they had hiked. She cut her treasures and took them home. After experimenting with them, she brought her friends the creamy residue of liquids that she had stewed and brewed. She taught them how to rub the lotion into the pores of their faces until their skin glowed and their lips sparkled with natural color. How she created the lotions and how she made her friends look more beautiful, they never knew. Marina never revealed her secrets.

After graduating from the lyceum in Spera, Marina studied chemistry at the University of Cluj and then went to Bucharest to work at the geriatric clinic with Dr. Anna Aslan, a celebrated scientist, who was experimenting with a new medicine—Gerovital H3.

Dr. Aslan believed that daily injections of procaine and benzoic acid could slow down the aging process. She even found a special treatment for sexual rejuvenation. She was so much in demand that the international set and politicians began to come to her institute. They needed to stay young and powerful, and Dr. Aslan became their guru, a legend, a hero; and Marina, her assistant, memorized it all.

Once Marina had settled in New York with Mica's help, she leased a studio in Greenwich Village and arranged her kitchen as a lab for scientific beauty. She mixed elixirs she had learned from Gypsies in Transylvania, and added a dab of collagen to retin-A. Then she mixed bee pollen with vitamin E and pulverized shark cartilage with honey. The result? A rejuvenating, regenerating, Romanian facial cream. She packaged it in golden ceramic hearts and marketed it as secret for lasting youth. She guaranteed romance and sold it for a fortune. Marina was a woman of scientific beauty—beauty that women wanted.

The four friends were truly independent and emancipated women. One might say they were women before their time, but that was not actually true. They just came from a different society than western women. The one advantage of an Eastern European and communist education was that all women and men were treated as equals. And for that reason, women were encouraged to achieve on the same level as their male counterparts, in any field they chose. As a result, the women had developed strong egos and self-confidence. The four friends had enjoyed the advantage of gender freedom in a communist regime that paradoxically limited all other freedoms. And each one in their own field had succeeded.

But what differentiated them was their looks. At five-foot-four and 110 pounds, Mica was the most petite. Yet she was far from frail. To the contrary, she was physically strong and a talented dancer. She had natural grace, carried herself lightly, and wore her dark hair short. Her face, an olive complexion, was complimented by beautiful almond-shaped hazel-green eyes that glowed golden, revealing a fire inside.

Anca was a head taller than Mica at five-foot-nine. She was thin and narrowly built, but strong in appearance, as if her compact body needed strength to study medicine and heal her patients. She was the cerebral power of the quartette, and they deferred to her for analysis. Studious and intellectual, she always had a book or newspaper or cellphone in her handbag. A photographic memory helped her remember details that were critical to her patients' health. She was a very good person and was always giving and helping others. Often, her friends warned her, she gave too much.

Cristina was the most beautiful of the four. As a fashion designer, her stylish clothes and mysterious allure enhanced her natural beauty. From the time she was a young girl, people had turned their heads to admire her. At a picture-perfect height of five-foot-eight, she wore high heels to give herself a willowy elegance. She was proud of her fiery-red hair, which she often wore long and wavy like Botticelli's Venus. At other times, she wore it in a chignon, like a royal crown. She had intense green eyes, and when she stared at someone, they'd often turn away, unsettled by the force of her look. Yet when she smiled, her face became sweet, and her kindness shone through. She was also the artist of the group, searching to find beauty where others dared not look.

Marina was the most imposing of the four Musketeers. Almost six feet tall in heels, her robust body was in proportion with her height. The German word for voluptuous to describe full-bodied red wines, *üppig,* fit Teutonic Marina as well. Beautiful in her own style, she wore her straight black hair in a chignon. Spending hours in her lab while experimenting with plants, she needed her hair out of her eyes. But in the evenings, when she'd dine and entertain, she unclipped her curls and let herself be free.

Marina was the most aggressive of the friends, and whenever action or words were needed, she'd move forward like a lion. It was natural for her to have become the entrepreneur of the group. However, she was also the most complex. She had a touch of naïveté despite her sophistication. She was kind and child-like, yet still had a tough business sense. It was this discrepancy of character that made her intriguing and highly charming. Yet despite her outward self-confidence, there was a sadness to her laugh. Marina was a mystery, and even her dear fiends didn't know everything about her. It was as if she lived with secrets, and working non-stop was her way to forget what was hidden inside.

The Four Musketeers were indeed poets of their lives, creating their existence. When they were teenagers, their greatest pleasure was to hike on Saturdays in the Carpathian Mountains. They'd walk in a line, holding hands, and sing, *We are the poets of our lives.*

The four women could look back on their many years of friendship and say they'd shared a full life together. And now, at sixty years old, full of energy and projects, they were still tasting the pleasures of each day and relishing being *one for all and all for one.*

Mica's world was complete. She loved her husband, André, and admired his work as a cardiologist, claiming he understood the most about the heart. Their twin sons, Craig and Michael, were working in fields they enjoyed. And of course, she had Luca, her adopted son, who was in his last year at Wharton and would be soon joining his biological mother, Andrea, for summer vacation in Transylvania. Andrea was now a radiologist at Cluj's university hospital.

Anca was equally satisfied with her life. She had found again the man she loved, Petre Ilianu. They'd settled in New York City, not far from Mica, where Anca practiced medicine and taught pediatrics at New York Hospital. Petre continued to work with the C.I.A. and with Eugen Simionescu, Cristina's husband. Together, they fought for justice, whether in post-communist Romania or other hotspots around the world. Sandra, their daughter, was married to a professor of International Relations at New York University where she also taught at the Law School. Their five-year-old daughter, Michelle, was Anca's passion. She called her *mi amor.*

Cristina had remained in Paris, where she and Eugen lived the high life. There was no political or social gathering without them. Eugen knew everyone involved in politics and counterintelligence, and Cristina knew everyone in France's social whirl. She continued each fashion season with a different type of show and was always searching for beauty that had never been seen before. It was through her creative designs that she had become a symbol of Parisian style.

Marina, the wealthiest of the Four Musketeers, had always been searching for the unknown. She lived to work, always wanting more challenges. Her research with plants and herbs had led her to question what could make women look more beautiful, feel younger, love better. Her entire life had been a search for the treasure of beauty. It was a quest that she'd shared with Cristina, and over the years, it had taken them both to the fascinating parts of the world.

Yet for Marina, the most secret treasure of all was happiness, and that had been more difficult to find.

# 4

*Santa Fe, New Mexico*
*March 27, 2017*

CRISTINA AND MARINA met at the car rental agency in Santa Fe's airport. After doing the necessary paperwork, they left in a red, four-wheel-drive jeep. Marina drove since Cristina was already having a headache from the high altitude.

"I've been reading about these mountains," Cristina commented. "Seems there's a treasure chest hidden somewhere near Taos."

"Taos?" Marina asked. "That's about 70 miles north of Santa Fe. We can hike there and try our luck." She laughed at the thought.

"It's a modern-day treasure hunt, set up by an art dealer from Santa Fe, Forrest Fenn. He claims he's hidden an antique treasure chest filled with gold coins, gold nuggets, and Native American artifacts. He wrote down clues to its location in twenty-four verses of a poem he included in his memoir, *The Thrill of the Chase.*"

"Do you actually believe that?" Marina asked skeptically.

"Of course." The artist in Cristina was intrigued by the story.

"He started the search after recovering from kidney cancer. Claimed that the greatest tragedy of life is not living it. So he created this treasure hunt. So people could chase dreams."

"Come on," Marina insisted. "How could a sophisticated woman like you believe that there's a hidden treasure chest? Must be a hoax. Maybe a *symbolic* treasure chest, okay, but not something *tangible.*"

"Not really. Look at our lives. The four of us. Each one of us escaped a Communist country and ventured into the world to fight for her own dream. And in our way, we each found our own treasure chest."

"You're right," Marina agreed, giving in to her friend's enthusiasm. "We should continue our adventures, no matter what our age. You're reminding me to believe my own publicity: *The heart doesn't age, nor does the soul. Age is only a number, a secret to behold.*"

Cristina laughed. "So we can stay young and beautiful forever!"

"That's my work! Maybe these mountains will lead us to a treasure I've been searching for—a fountain of youth. Weren't the Spanish explorers searching for it in these very mountains?"

"Yes, Coronado came to New Mexico in the 16th century to find that fountain, but he was also looking for gold. He said the area was one of the Seven Cities of Gold." Cristina laughed at the idea. "I'll have to tell this to Eugen. He let it slip out yesterday that he's going back and forth to New York City, coordinating an investigation with Petre about a gold smuggler from Turkey. He suspects that the leaders of Turkey and Iran lured some talented young men to work with them, and then the governments turned against them."

"Beware of that old Romanian saying: *Today's friend, tomorrow's fall guy.*"

"According to Eugen, the American government is trying to find out who the gold belonged to originally. The death of Iranian,

Rafsanjani, has roiled the waters. I guess my husband and Anca's are on their own treasure hunt."

"Let's hope it doesn't take a dangerous twist," Marina stated.

"I hope there are no surprises. Turkey can be Byzantine–secretive. Even Istanbul is that way, filled with underground caves. Dark and mysterious. Like the catacombs in Paris," Cristina commented, and then continued telling her story.

"The Taos pueblo, where this treasure hunt starts, is at the base of a mountain range called the Sangre de Cristos."

"Doesn't *sangre* mean blood?" Marina interrupted.

"Yes. You're not squeamish, are you?"

"Me? No..."

"Well, the pueblo has a unique type of architecture—four-story houses made of adobe that are built into rocks. You need a rope ladder from the ground to climb up and down. There are no steps to enter or leave, no electricity, no water, no plumbing, no heat, no toilets, no phones, no internet. That's why only a few dozen devoted Tanoans live in the pueblo. That's the name of the people from the tribe."

"Sounds fascinating," Marina commented.

"There are 4,500 natives today who live outside the pueblo throughout their reservation of 95,000 acres. The Tanoans are known to be very private, very determined to preserve their traditions. They believe they live on sacred land."

"Aha! And that's where the golden treasure is located?"

"Yes, according to eighty-seven-year-old Forrest Fenn in his memoir."

"Did he make this up for fun?" Marina asked.

"No—to give people the chance to have fun!"

"I'm sold!" Marina said in her business tone. "We begin tomorrow morning after a good night's rest." Then she slowed her driving down. "Look on the right. We've arrived at the Inn. My secretary said it's the best in town, the only Relais & Châteaux."

"I thought you wanted to rough it."

"Of course!" Marina assured her. "We'll rough it just as soon as we sleep in luxury and breakfast in plenty."

As they approached the Inn, they noticed it was located opposite Santa Fe's oldest jail.

"Are you sure this is it?" Cristina questioned. "Looks modest from the outside."

"Patience, *ma chère*. Maybe it's an omen for our trip—*search deeper to find a treasure.*"

---

After climbing a few steps to the office, they walked into the bright glare of the setting sun. Next to the reception area was an outdoor garden, occupied by a tent made from fabrics of different colors and designs. Inside the tent was a wooden swing, painted with colored geometric patterns that matched the outside fabrics. Two large silk cushions embroidered with golden flowers, covered the ground around the swing.

Cristina picked up one of the cushions to admire it, when a tall, woman with long blond hair, came over to greet them. Her words were slightly accented with a mixture of German and British. Strongly built and imposing, she wore several strands of beaded turquoise Indian necklaces with sea shells and dangling, turquoise earrings. Her face was taut and lined by years of sun and mountain air. She reminded one of Alfred Stieglitz's photos of Georgia O'Keefe in a certain way.

"My name is Gretchen. Welcome to our Inn. Let me offer you a refreshing drink made from local fruit and herbs." She handed them each a glass of juice topped with red currants and mint leaves. "This will help you acclimate to the altitude."

"Thank you. I do feel a bit light-headed," Cristina confessed.

"It can take a day or two to get used to. Drink plenty of liquids, but no alcohol. You may want to rest before dinner."

"Good idea," Cristina agreed, looking westward as the sun was beginning to set.

"But first, please take a seat in this swing for two," Gretchen said. "It turns toward the sun, like a sunflower." And she demonstrated how it moved automatically with the help of a silent motor.

Cristina and Marina sat in the swing and sipped their drinks, relaxing and chatting as the sun created bursts of red, orange, yellow, and purple on the blue sky. The colors of the late-day sun were reflected on the garden's white stucco walls.

"Whenever I see such beauty, I get a little sad," Marina confessed.

"Sad? Why? It should make you happy."

"Logically, yes. But I can't convince the demons that are inside me to be logical. I remember the beautiful winter days in our Carpathian Mountains when I'd walk alone in the snow. It was all white—pure—the mountains, the sky, the air in front of me—and I'd feel sad. Beauty is hard to find and it lasts such a short time."

"Please, Marina, your deep thoughts are making me sad. Let's change the topic. Let's talk about something more cheerful."

"Fine. Choose your subject."

"Let's talk about love. That will change your thoughts," Cristina said.

"No, better yet, let's talk about sex. That may even make us laugh. You start. You're living in gay Paris. The city of pleasures—food, wine, fashion. Sex too. The temptation of life. Forbidden fruit."

"No, you start, Marina. Your idea. And to hear your story about sex will remind me when we were teenagers and we'd chat about sex and love for hours. Please, free yourself and tell me all. All."

"You win," said Marina. She took a deep breath and began:

"Once upon a time in a country called Romania, there were no pleasures, no freedom, no food, but lots of sex. That's where I discovered for the first time the joy of making love."

"You're preparing me for a juicy story."

"I was eighteen, the September of beginning the university. You remember how I wore my black hair long and straight down to my waist?"

"You were strikingly beautiful. I remember you had your own style, especially your tight sweaters, around the bust." They both laughed.

"I was ripe. But Ceausescu had forbidden condoms. We couldn't get them or afford them on the black market. I didn't want to get pregnant. You remember Greta Iliona during high school?"

"What a horror. Abortions were illegal and so dangerous. What a bloody way to die. Poor girl. And her parents…"

"That marked all of us. Curtailed our sex drive. What a pity that abortions were cheaper than contraceptives."

"I remember that a doctor would perform an abortion for a bottle of wine. So, tell me, how were you brave enough to have sex in such a hell?"

"I began as a woman of the book. In a place of books."

"Now you're giving me clues. Like our treasure hunt. Sex was the treasure?"

"What could be a better treasure at eighteen? I went to the university library. Found the book *Kama Sutra*, an ancient Sanskrit treatise in Hindi about lessons of love, which was translated in Romanian as *Desire Soul*. I must confess the book had been defaced from overuse. I hid it among my large sketch pads of plants and herbs. I was afraid to be seen with it, or even to check it out with the librarian."

"Such a serious student."

"Curious. Creative."

They laughed, enjoying being together, two dear friends,

watching the sun set, chatting and enjoying each other as they had when they were so very young.

"After I studied the book in the bathroom, I made some sketches of the most fascinating positions. Then I went to the main lobby and looked at every guy who entered or left. I was thinking if I'm going to start my sex life, it has to be with someone I like physically. I told myself you must *choose your type.*"

"What type was that?"

"Handsome with the ideal male body. Remember, I'm an admirer of beauty. So after standing near the door for more than thirty minutes, studying every male face and pair of legs, I saw the right man come in. He was alone, fulfilling prerequisite one—he'd keep the secret from his friends. He was carrying several books, prerequisite two—intelligent. It was a warm day. He was wearing a t-shirt, emphasizing his strong but slender chest. He wore shorts that exposed muscular legs. Blond hair, long and free, His full lips were a good sign, sensual. Clean shaven and neat—prerequisite three, no diseases. About twenty years old—prerequisite four, probably experienced, at least more than me."

"You sound like a scientist doing research or preparing an experiment. You were always so methodical. How did you begin your conversation with your Roman god?"

"I introduced myself and asked him if I could invite him for coffee."

"He must have felt struck by Cupid's arrow."

"Not yet. I tried to keep it purely academic. After the smiles, I showed him the book I was reading. Just the cover, with two naked bodies embracing. That said it all. I didn't want to check out the book, still afraid I'd be caught, and yet I was not ready to give it up. So we stayed in the building with the book and my sketches, and took the steps downstairs. He followed me to the coffee shop.

"I told him I was a student of botany, and in order to under-stand plants, I needed to understand biology. But most of all, I was a student of philosophy, and I needed to free myself from bour-geois values."

"He must have thought you were a true Communist. Surprising he didn't think you worked for the Secret Police, sent to trap him for a trumped-up reason. Amazing he trusted you."

"I explained that I needed to understand the human body and correlate similarities with the plant world. To make a comparative study of mutual physical elements."

"Did he understand what you were getting at?"

"Not at first; and yet in a way, yes. He was a medical student, and he agreed that understanding the physical could lead to an emotional harmony, a spiritual liberation."

Cristina laughed. "Your soul mate."

"I showed him my sketches related to lovemaking from different angles. I asked if he was curious? Interested in following the book?"

"He must have thought you were crazy."

Marina laughed, her full body laugh. "I spoke very seriously. He took my hand and asked me if I had a place for us to make my sketches come alive. I answered no. He said the med school has a study room. He could get the key from a friend who had the right to use it in exchange for some research he was doing."

"Are you making up this story?"

"No! I'm trying to remember something beautiful."

"And then?"

"We returned the book to its place on the shelf and left together to the med school. Georgi, that was his name, found his friend, got the key, and then we were alone in the study room. It smelled strange, of old books. There was very little light, but we found some candles and lit them. There were also several chairs and a couch. Georgi locked the door. We took off our clothes. We had to be quiet, which was fine, for we were busy touching each other. It was all very exciting. Such high risk. I loved the dare. And with someone I didn't even know."

"And Georgi?"

"He was very excited also. It was bliss—a climax of sheer abandon, not thinking of anything but pleasure. Our coming together at the same time was religious, divine, uniting our souls."

"Did you and Georgi keep seeing each other?"

"How could we not? We were hooked. Sex became our drug. We became more and more daring,"

"What happened?"

"We became obsessed with inventing all kinds of ways to have climaxes together. Front, back, side, anal, oral, upside down, like acrobats. There were sixty-four positions in the book. We kept referring to it and tried all of them—playing like children—rocking horse, crossed legs, tumbling. It was a frenzy of sensuality! And all the time amidst high risk. Georgi was searching for condoms but had found none, so we were putting a great deal at stake. Yet all we could think of was that we wanted more and more."

"Marina, what a wild side of you I never knew!"

"After a couple of months, Georgi was finally able to get condoms. They were selling them on the black market for a cheaper price. The government changed the policy because sexual diseases were becoming rampant.

"We'd meet twice a week, very late at night in the same room. It went on for an entire year until Georgi finished med school and was transferred to another city for his internship."

"Wow! How lucky you were to have experienced such beautiful sex!" And then Cristina said in a hurt tone, "You never told me about this." She and Marina had sworn never to hide secrets from each other. Musketeers.

"You were busy at art school, already designing clothes. We

didn't see each other again until we both went to Germany with Mica's help and were busy negotiating with her lawyers."

"Yes, other challenges. Did you ever see Georgi again?"

"No, but I think of him often, when I see something very beautiful, like this sunset, that I know won't last. And it makes me think of my first time making love. Something that was so beautiful, but didn't last. I was blessed to have had that relationship so young. We were free at a time when freedom was forbidden. We truly wanted to give pleasure to each other. Unselfishly. Tenderly. It was a beautiful beginning."

"Of sex?"

"No, of hope. If you're free in sex, free from bourgeois values, you have hope that life has lots of pleasures. Life can be wonderful if you go out and search for what's special and not be afraid to find it. After such an experience, I was able to love stronger, because I remembered how much I was loved and could give love. I could never forget that. It gave me self-confidence so I could go on in life and not be afraid. Loving and being loved gave me courage."

# 5

*Santa Fe, New Mexico*
*March 27, 2017*

GRETCHEN RETURNED at the same second the sky turned dark, the magic had disappeared. The friends' closeness would have to wait for another time—maybe for Cristina's story—when she was ready to open up and talk about how she began.

"Let me lead you to your room," Gretchen told the women. "Night will soon turn cool."

She led them down several steps from the reception area into the street. When she opened the door of their suite, there was a sculpted glass chandelier of deep turquoise that colored the white walls to a brilliant blue-green.

"A design from Chihuly," Gretchen said proudly. "This is our best room."

The furniture was covered with similar fabrics as had been used on the tent and swing. Cristina walked over to the couch and caressed the gold-threaded, embroidered flowers. "I've never seen or felt a fabric like this before," she said. "It seems to be made with a special raw silk and gold stitching."

Gretchen smiled. "The fabric was made for us. Fourteen-karat gold thread. That's why the stitching looks golden."

"I hope it's not smuggled gold," Cristina said, laughing at her private joke.

"Smuggle gold? How would one do that?" she asked, laughing.

"I'll let you know next week when I see my husband." But suddenly Cristina wasn't joking or smiling anymore. Instead, she was massaging her forehead. Gretchen noticed Cristina's discomfort and kindly said, "I can send some medicine for your headache with the bellboy, along with your bags. Or I can give it to your friend, if she accompanies me to my office."

"Of course," Marina responded. "Might be faster if I follow you."

As the women were walking toward the office, Gretchen asked her, "Are you from New York City?"

"Yes. And Cristina is from Paris."

"Well, in New York, there's the most fascinating legal-political case going on now."

"You mean the gold laundering scandal?"

"Yes. I'm addicted to spy thrillers, and this case should be written up in a book."

"You're right—life and literature intermingling together to become one."

"They've been giving daily updates in a modern way: through apps, podcasts, blogs, videos. The world can come right into your home these days."

"No more secrets. We have to be careful." Marina smiled with the thought.

"My favorite podcast is *D.A. Crimes and Scandals*," Gretchen commented. "It's once a week. Two young women in Sweden sit in front of a camera and discuss international crimes. They've created a platform with a million viewers from around the globe. Their subject for the past few weeks has been this gas-for-gold case. If you're interested, you can join it."

"I would love to! How?"

"I can have my technician register and sign you up. I have your contact information at the desk."

"Cristina too? I'll get her hooked on the case."

"I can also register you both for a vlog that has daily transmissions."

"You mean a blog?"

"No, *vlog*—from Finland. A combination of video and blog with audio. Something like YouTube but more private. Not for everyone. They give daily updates on the case. Let me show you."

Gretchen took out her cell phone and logged into the site. A video image came up, and she showed it to Marina. "Wait a minute before I start it. Let me arrange first to send your friend her medicine. I don't want her to wait for you."

"Good idea."

Gretchen spoke to the bellman and then turned her attention back to Marina. "This transmission comes from Helsinki."

*Dear viewers, the question we ask about this case, is why did Turkey pay Iran for gas in gold?"*

*The answer is easy: Turkey could not pay Iran with dollars or euros because those currencies were traceable as going against the sanctions, and clearly, breaking international law. In addition, for Turkey to pay in their currency—Turkish lira—was not acceptable to Iran, because that currency is weak and has limited value in global markets. So Iran insisted that Turkey should pay in gold. This meant that Turkey had to first transfer their lira to gold, and that is what Sharatt did. He made the currency transfer, based on his past experience, by moving the Turkish lira to his shell companies. Then he paid Iran in the form of physical gold--gold bullion bars.*

*Let's return to the beginning of the case in 2011. If Turkey circumvents sanctions and goes against international law and pays Iran in gold, it helps Iran's economy. Gold is a strong currency and difficult to trace. In addition, Turkey gets a better price for the gas and oil, which makes Ozogant, who was Prime Minister then, look good.*

*Ozogant wanted to be elected President in 2014 after being Prime Minister for eleven years. An increase in the economy would show he could manage the budget and Finances as president.*

*The next question that intrigues us, is why, would a man as clever as Sharatt come to Miami and risk getting caught? Didn't he know he'd be arrested? The F.B.I. has had him on record since 2013. They had judged him guilty in absentia because he used banks registered in New York as conduits for this gas-for-gold scheme.*

*We suspect that Sharatt wanted to be arrested so he could make a deal directly with the American government. A deal to trade his information for a permanent visa to relocate in the States. That's why Ozogant wants him extradited. He's afraid he'll talk too much. I presume that Sharatt knows a lot about Ozogant and his family. But Sharatt doesn't trust the Turkish government. He told authorities at his arrest in Miami that his interests may not coincide with the interests of the Turkish Republic.*

*We believe that he went to the U.S. to stay alive. This was his*
*biggest scheme.It will be interesting to see how he achieves it.*

---

Marina knocked on the door, heard a "yes," and entered the room.

"Did you get the medicines?" she asked Cristina. "Feeling better?

"I took the medicines, but I'm still under the weather. I need another day to get better."

"Until then, to entertain you, I have a video to show you. A podcast about that gold case I was telling you about. It's amazing how the world is so small and news so accessible. Gretchen's interested in the same case, and she gave me access to some digital news. Each day there's an update. I registered you also if you want to follow. Look at this one from Sweden."

Marina took out her phone and clicked on the link Gretchen had shown her:

*We would like to share with our viewers some new information*
*about the accused. It's related to the fact that banks in New York*
*are involved in this case and why the Manhattan D.A.'s office*
*filed for Sharatt's arrest going back to 2013.*

*The C.I.A. and the F.B.I. are working with the Southern District*
*D.A.'s office on Sharatt's indictment. There are documents to*
*confirm that on December 17, 2013, Sharatt registered and signed*
*for a cargo plane that was flying from Accra, Ghana to Dubai.*
*But the plane was diverted to Istanbul's International airport*
*because of fog.*

*When a customs official searched the plane in Istanbul, he found*
*3,000 pounds of gold in bullion bars, along with false custom's*

paperwork. Sharatt was piloting the plane, and was arrested. The custom's official contacted the police chief in charge of corruption who, in turn, contacted an honest prosecutor to investigate the case. They learned that Sharatt had paid $63 million dollars in bribes to ministers in Ozogant's government. The investigation continued to Ozogant's house, which the prosecutor ordered to be secretly searched to see if he had received some of the money. They found a taped phone call between Ozogant and his son, Belcan, which the F.B.I. has a copy of.

Father told son to get rid of the cash in the house. But we hear Belcan, speaking in a desperate voice, explaining that after giving away millions of euros to family members, there was still 30 million euros in shoeboxes. He didn't know who else to give the money to.

The wiretaps with President Ozogant's voice could be proof that the president is one of Sharatt's accomplices.

What was the result of the investigation?

Ozogant got Sharatt released from jail with his accomplices who were aboard the plane with him. They are sons of government ministers. The Finance Minister, who was also involved, resigned, appearing to be embarrassed. But Ozogant kept him near and put him into Parliament. Others were not so lucky, including the custom's official who was forced to retire, and the chief of police who was exiled to a remote post in Turkey. And what happened to the honest prosecutor in Ankara? He was jailed.

As a summary to today's podcast analysis, we would like to remind our viewers that the revenue for Iran and Turkey during the years of this scandal, came to $11 billion per year, from the dates being investigated, 2011 to 2015. We calculate that this is a total sum of $55 billion. That's a lot of money. And who took the lion's share?

We leave our viewers with this last thought and will return tomorrow with more breaking news.

# 6

*Santa Fe, New Mexico*
*March 27, 2017*

IT WAS early morning in Santa Fe and Marina was driving the red jeep with the hood down toward Taos. She was alone, for Cristina had awakened with the same splitting headache. Cristina assured Marina that the pain would pass and that they'd hike together the next day to search for the treasure. She opted to stay at the hotel and make some work-related phone calls to Paris, and then in the afternoon, said that she'd stroll into town. She insisted that Marina shouldn't worry about her, but go and explore the mountains on her own.

Gretchen had advised Marina to take the route north following the signs to the Sangre de Cristo mountains. She gave her a map where she'd marked the route in yellow and circled the section before Blue Lake.

"In the beginning, your car can enter, but then the road gets rocky. You'll see a parking lot on the left." She colored the road in yellow and circled the place where Marina should leave her car—in front of a large cactus bush.

"It's a hike of about three miles to Blue Lake. After an hour of walking, you'll see a sign with the word "PRIVATE." Stop there. The area around the lake is only for members of the tribe. In 1996, President Nixon decreed that the land belonged to the Tanoans. Everyone agrees the area has spiritual powers."

Marina gave her a quizzical look.

"Use your compass or GPS. The trail isn't marked."

Driving through the mountains, Marina felt the morning air turn suddenly cool. Her ears began to feel blocked, and she noticed a sign, ALTITUDE: 10,000 FEET. She saw the parking lot, remarked that hers was the only car, and rationalized, "It's early."

She parked in the shadow of the cactus and took from the trunk a backpack that Gretchen had given her containing a canteen of water, a Swiss Army knife, a first aid kit, binoculars, and compass. She unclipped her hair and let her black curls hang straight to her shoulders—free. Dressed in beige hiking pants, a white turtle neck sweater, hiking boots, and wide brimmed straw hat, she looked like a Manhattan tourist ready for anything in the desert.

She walked to the side of the parking lot, where a sharp cliff opened up to a wide vista of remarkable beauty. Stretched before her was a panorama of unending mountains. Between the ranges, she noticed small flocks of white birds flying against a blue sky. It reminded her of the Atlas Mountains in Morocco, her last trip with Stefan.

She stopped walking, took a deep breath and thought of Stefan, the husband she'd loved so much and had lost too young to cancer. She wiped tears from her eyes, kicked some rocks, and tried to focus on good thoughts: the beauty of the land before her—mountain and desert living side by side—a little like she felt at night dreaming of Stefan, wanting him, but finding instead a dusty path.

She tried to change her thoughts and concentrate on the nature surrounding her.

The landscape was hardly believable, it was so varied. She didn't know where to look first. Slowly, her eyes found the Sangre de Cristo mountain range high above her and a trail that descended to the desert floor. Intrigued, she eyed a lower path that looked interesting to explore. She breathed in deeply and the smell of mesquite rejuvenated her.

She climbed downward, often slipping on the rocky floor, until the mountains disappeared and all she had before her were dozens of cacti of varying texture and sizes. As she hiked on, she walked through columns of strange rock formations; jagged pillars reflecting the sun in shades of burnt red and brown. Curious to see more, she took a small foot path and trampled on spiny bushes that were brittle like bone. The morning sun had burned off the mountain chill, and its glare penetrated her face. Heat baked her clothes; she started to sweat. Yellow jackets began to follow her perfumed trail.

She passed a group of senita cacti and a patch of cat's claw, scrubby bushes with long spines and sharp bristles. The curved claws clung to her pants and held her back. She hesitated and pulled her legs free. She felt as if she were traveling through a world where no person had ever dared tread before. As she wandered, the desert felt less threatening and its beauty captivated her with its secrets. Frailty and strength lived side by side. It was frightening yet magical, and intrigued, she trekked on.

Suddenly, Marina realized she wasn't alone. From a mesquite bush came noise and movement. A man appeared. At first she thought she must be seeing a mirage. He was very tall, with a thin frame, and wide, strong shoulders. He was middle-aged, with a weathered, suntanned face and long gray hair that reached to his shoulders. He was wearing a white Stetson hat, khaki pants, and a khaki shirt. He looked like he came from a time when cowboys had roamed the Wild West. Marina also noticed that he carried a revolver strapped tight to his hip.

"Howdy," he greeted her and smiled. "Where you going?"

She hesitated to answer, afraid she might be trespassing. Gretchen had told her not to venture near Blue Lake—that it was private, sacred land.

"I was hiking, but it's getting hot, and I thought I should return to my car in the parking lot."

"The one near the sign TRAILS? Where the land is a strange mixture of mountain and desert?"

"Yes, but I'm not sure about the direction." She took the compass off her neck and tried to assess where she was and how to return to where she had started.

"Wouldn't want you to get lost in these trails. Best to go towards the left, not right. That wouldn't be right."

"How do I get there?"

"Well, hard to explain. Left at the boojum tree, right at the creeping devil, another left at the milkweed, and left again at the squaw bush. Look for the desert willow, twenty feet tall."

"What's all that?" She smiled to hide her uncertainty.

"Not easy to find. Mind if I walk with you? I'll show you the way."

Eyeing the revolver shining in the sun, she hesitated and replied with a stutter, "I-I can find it."

"It's a hard one. These lands change fast. Not always friendly. My pleasure to help."

Pointing to the ground to prove his point, he added, "Look at the kangaroo rat carrying a lizard in its mouth. And look at the red ants chasing the lizard." Then he pointed to a yellow jacket flying near her neck. "He likes your perfume."

She didn't know if he was giving her a compliment and if she should smile or not, when suddenly the insect bit the nape of her neck. She tried to slam it with her hand, but all she hit was her hair and neck, and she yelled in pain. "Oh no! It stung me! It hurts!"

"Don't move," he said and quickly bent down to the ground, took a handful of dirt, and sprinkled several drops of water from his canteen into his dirty hand. "Don't be afraid."

She eyed his hand full of mud and attempted to move away and stop him, but before she could say no, he lifted her hair and rubbed the back of her neck with his muddy palm.

"Wait, I need to give you more." He repeated his movements and rubbed her neck again. The sting and pain disappeared as suddenly as they had begun.

"What did you do?"

"Just a local remedy. Glad it helped."

"I can't thank you enough." She smiled at him as if he were a magician. And staring at him, she also realized how handsome he was, in a very unusual way.

"I'm pleased to meet you," she said, extending her hand. "My name is Marina."

"I'm Tahquitz."

"Are you Native American? From the Tanoan tribe?"

"Yes, but you know, I still call myself an Indian. My great-great grandfather was the chief. They called him Elk. My people are part of the Plains Indians, like the Cheyennes and Apaches. But we broke away. Different beliefs. We're Catholics. And we have the sacred Blue Lake. The only water in the middle of the desert."

"The mud that you put on my neck... is that what you'd call Indian medicine?"

"Yes. I studied western medicine at med school in Denver. Did my internship and residency there in pediatrics. After that, I returned to my tribe to take care of the children..." He paused a second, looked down, took a deep breath, and continued.

"Then I saw patients of all ages with our shaman until he passed away. That's how I learned Indian medicine—from him."

Marina was both curious and impressed. She twisted her neck to test its mobility, told him she was fine, and thanked him again.

"Glad you're better. I'll lead you out."

They walked and talked. She asked questions—"I always wondered, what exactly is a shaman?"—and he explained.

"A shaman understands that everything in the world is part of our Great Spirit."

"You mean God?"

"Not exactly. The Great Spirit has an inner power that's linked to nature that has a healing strength. The shaman works in harmony with herbs and plants that have medicinal powers."

Marina stared at him, yet she understood what he was saying. It was not unlike what she did with her beauty creams—plants that have power.

"In our tribe," he continued, "there are two sorts of healers. One, a medical doctor, trained in western medicine, who takes care of children and adults. And then there's a shaman, sometimes called a medicine man. He tends to the spiritual needs of the tribe. Takes away the pain that's inside." He pointed to his heart. "His powers are given to him by the Great Spirit and revealed to him in a vision quest."

"What's that?"

"First, one must ask, *who* goes on a vision quest? It should be someone who is part of the founding family and who chooses to live the life of responsibility to the tribe."

"I imagine that was you."

"Yes. The vision quest was a mission for me to find spiritual strength. I left the tribe, and fasted and prayed for three days in these mountains. I was waiting for a sign from the Great Spirit. On the third night, it came to me in a dream. I saw the Great Spirit in the form of a bear, and he spoke to me."

Marina was trying hard to believe his tale. She wanted to believe it was true and not just a story.

"He told me to treat my people with both western and tribal medicine. Be their bridge and healer."

"Is that what you did?"

"Not right away. I went first to the holy man of our tribe so he could interpret my dream and advise me. He led me through a series of purifying ceremonies and blessings to protect me from bad spirits. Then he told me I was chosen by the Great Spirit to assist the elderly shaman. So that's what I did."

She thought of Roma—the Gypsies—she had known in Transylvania. There was something magical about their powers. In fact, she often used their secrets in her beauty creams.

"He taught me the importance of maintaining a balance between man's inner spirit and the outside world. If not, man will be unhappy. He won't have peace."

Marina was captivated by his words and by the timbre of his voice, melodious and strong, confidant, and reassuring. He spoke like a poet, a preacher, a mystic. Was there a chemical attraction pulling her toward this man because of the spiritual strength emanating from him? She tried to control her emotional reaction and thought perhaps she could learn from him. If the mountains had secrets, he must understand them. But before she could ask a question, he continued talking.

"My grandfather taught me everything I know. He'd visit the people of our tribe on Sundays and take me with him— to church, to the pueblo, to their homes—from the time I was seven years old." He smiled proudly. "He'd explain to me about our tribe—our customs, rituals, plants, animals. It was very exciting for me to be with him."

"How lucky you were," Marina said, feeling slightly bad that she had not known either of her grandfathers. They had been killed in wars. "Tell me about him, please. I'm interested."

"One day, when he took me for a hike in these mountains, he saw a small spring on the ground, bubbling like a geyser, and above it was a rapid waterfall. He put the water from the waterfall inside his canteen and the next day, had the water analyzed. It contained important minerals like calcium, magnesium, and potassium. He found other springs in these mountains and other waterfalls and set up centers where the spring water was pure. He gave the water to our people and guarded the springs and their secrets until he decided what would be the next step."

She listened, holding on to his words, feeling the vibrancy of his thoughts and feelings. She moved closer.

Tahquitz continued talking, absorbed in remembering. "My grandfather read about spring water in Europe and took a trip to Evian, France to learn how they bottle the water there. Our tribe has an agreement with the American government that we don't pay taxes on the earnings from our land—and the tribe made a fortune with the bottling and distribution of the spring water. My grandfather put all the money into a scholarship foundation."

"I can understand why you're so proud of him."

"Yes, he taught me a lot. I spent a great deal of time working with him and the foundation."

"How lucky you were to have him." Marina was fascinated by Tahquitz's story.

"Over the years, he taught me secrets he had learned from nature—secrets he'd found in the land of the Tanoan people." He stretched his long arms outward, and she remembered the sculpture of Christ in Brazil, on top of Corcovado Mountain in Rio de Janeiro. She and Stefan had taken a trip together there, right after working on their first successful cream lotion, to celebrate... She wanted to stop thinking of Stefan. Why was she thinking so much of him today?

"What area of study are you interested in?" Tahquitz asked. Marina thought he had sensed her mood change and kindly wanted to cheer her up.

"Beauty. Youth." She couldn't help herself from blurting it out.

She hoped it didn't sound superficial to him. He was talking about things deeper than beauty, and he looked so comfortable in his rugged, natural manliness.

Tahquitz laughed. "You can't find miracles out there," he said, pointing toward the mountain range, "if you've got nothing in here." His long finger pointed again to his heart. "Age is not counted by numbers."

She smiled. "I agree. But how do *you* count age?"

"One thing's for sure—age comes quickly with stress." And he stretched his arms again, far above the Sangre de Cristo peaks.

"Are there any plants in your land that can help reduce stress?" she asked.

"Sure. Narcotic-inducing plants. Hallucinogens, too—but no good. They destroy the mind, take away one's will and leave a person empty."

"I understand. But are there plants to make you feel younger?" Marina was feeling excited. The sun shone on Tahquitz's bronzed skin, highlighting his sculpted high cheekbones. There was a sparkle in his hazel eyes, a smile on his face, inviting and mischievous. She couldn't stop looking at him.

"I think you want some secrets from me," he said smiling. "Do you want to stay beautiful forever?" he teased.

"That would be fun."

"I don't know if plants could achieve that forever." He clapped his hands and laughed. She felt his joy and she felt happy.

"We do have herbs that stop balding and make your hair fuller," he said. "That may help you look younger. Feel younger, too."

"Yes," she smiled, remembering her mentor, Dr. Aslan, who experimented for years to find a lotion to stop balding. What fun it had been for her and Stefan to work together in her lab in Bucharest. One year after that, Marina left Romania for West Germany and Stefan followed her, escaping in a daring way. One night, when she had lost hope that he was safe, he appeared at the door of her studio lab in New York. There they worked and loved for ten years, until.…

"Are these plants here?" She wanted to stop thinking of Stefan. "Can you point them out to me?"

"Sure." He took out his knife and cut a piece of cactus. Sticky, thick white sap flowed into his hand. "Like aloe and yucca, but better," he explained, showing her. "Not just for burns, but to hydrate the skin. Used against balding because it penetrates deep into several layers to keep the scalp moist, so hair follicles are nourished and grow. Stress dries the scalp. Skin too."

She stared at him, his knowledge, his wisdom, passion. "Smells like mesquite." She didn't know what else to say.

"That's right," he smiled. "Look at this." He bent down to pick up a crawling vine from a bush. Breaking the leaves, he put several white flower pieces to her nose. "What does this smell like?"

"Coconut."

"Desert coconut. Skunk bush. Works just like coconut oil from the tropics. Rub it on your teeth and gums."

She took the fine pieces and massaged her gums with them. "It tastes sweet, but feels rough."

"My people use it instead of toothpaste to whiten the teeth." He smiled and displayed a full set of brilliant, white teeth. "Helps the gums, too—it stops bleeding. We make a liquid from boiling the stems."

He picked up a stick from a willow tree and pointed to plants as they walked."Look at this one." It was tiny, brown, and grainy. At first she thought it was a piece of earth.

"I mix this with olive oil and salt and rub it into a lesion on the skin or a burn. Better than aloe. It works faster and doesn't leave a scar."

He bent down and picked up another vine from a bush. Breaking the leaves, he put several white flower pieces to her nose.

"Digitalis, also called foxglove. Take a bud. We boil it for tea. It helps control heart rate. I see some bristles stuck on your pants." He bent down and removed them from her legs. When he touched her, she felt her body turn warm. She didn't move, and closed her eyes.

"You see that thorny scrub bush, over yonder?" He pointed with his stick. "The one with the red leaves. We use the berry for tea to improve blood flow. Rejuvenates and gives your cheeks a rosy glow." He smiled at her and his eyes lingered on hers.

"These are the treasures from my tribe's garden."

She wanted to move closer to him, yet held herself back. Before she could say or do anything else, she saw her red jeep.

"Looks like we found the right trail," he said and took her hand with the intention of saying good bye. But he held it several seconds and softly caressed her skin with his fingers. A strange sensation flowed through her body, as if their hands were making a special contact. They looked into each other's eyes and smiled.

"Are you in town tomorrow?" he asked in a soft whisper. "Perhaps we can hike again?"

"Yes. I'd like that very much." And then she hesitated. "Is it a problem if my friend joins us..."

"Not at all. I've had so much fun."

## 7

*Taos, New Mexico*
*March 28, 2017*

MARINA DROVE toward Taos while Cristina chatted. "It was meant to be that I had a headache yesterday."

"Really?" Marina said. She was thinking the same thing. "Why do you say that?" Marina knew why she believed it—Tahquitz.

"Well," said Cristina, "Gretchen was so nice. After lunch, she offered to show me the town. Her husband has this amazing store. It's filled with treasures from all over the Middle East and Asia—carpets from Afghanistan, furniture from Azerbaijan, chests from Tibet, and above all, fabrics from Turkey. He works with a factory in Istanbul where fabrics are made from raw silk, gold threads and embroidered designs, all hand-sewn. I've never seen anything like it!"

"It looks like you found inspiration for a new fashion show. How about a parade of beautiful models wearing fezzes? And each one with a different colored Ali Baba pants and a sexy bare midriff?"

"Not a bad idea. Just what Paris needs. Her husband said Turkey is becoming a major textile manufacturer. You once spoke about going there. Maybe we should?"

"Why not? I hear the city has an ancient world of its own-- underground."

"*An underground city?*" Cristina asked.

"Yes. Built centuries ago to solve Istanbul's problem of over- flowing cemeteries. Millions of bones can still be found in the caves today."

"I wouldn't want to be stuck in a cave and my bones found there! Sounds like a nightmare. Let's change the subject," Cristina suggested.

"I made an appointment for the end of the day to meet the people who invited me to Santa Fe to sample their new facial creams. Would you like to join me?" Marina asked.

"Of course," and then Cristina started laughing. "After I visited town, I stopped in the square to buy an ice cream cone and rest. I turned to your podcast from Sweden–the one that summarizes the gold laundering case once a week."

"Yes?" Marina smiled, pleased her friend was hooked on the news.

"Like you said, this case is mesmerizing. It's highly addictive. At first, it's hard to believe it's real, and then it's hard to stop following it."

Cristina took her cell phone and secured it to the bracket on the dashboard. "Let me put it on while you drive. I'll turn up the audio to the max."

"Good. We have at least thirty minutes until we get to Taos."

The transmission was from Stockholm, featuring the two young women chatting with each other about the case. The tech- nology was so clear that it seemed as if the women were in the car talking to them.

*To summarize the gas for gold scandal, we turn to an analysis of Iran's partnership with Turkey.*

*We know that President Ozogant has a son, Belcan. They work very closely together, not in government, but privately. Let's say, in family business.*

*Belcan Ozogant has a good friend—Recep Sharatt. They also work in business together. And they have another good friend, Balal Zanssany, Iranian, who works with them in Tehran, on the other side of the scheme. This is Mr. Zanssany.*

His photo flashed on the screen.

*It's interesting to note that Recep Sharatt was born in Tabriz, Iran, to a well-connected family. This facilitated his joining an Iranian network that circumvented Iranian sanctions. One must look to Iranian Zanssany to understand the scheme.*

*Zanssany was arrested by the Iranians on December 30, 2013, for not paying the Iranian government $2.7 billion.*

*The Ministry of Petroleum claimed that Zanssany, as a broker and representative of the Iranian government, sold millions of barrels of Iranian oil on behalf of the Iranian government as their official middleman. The government couldn't sell it directly because of the embargo, so Zanssany did it for them from other countries by using a group of front companies. This generated a total of $17.5 billion for the Ministry of Oil. But Zanssany didn't turn over everything and owed the Iranian government $2.7 billion.*

*Zanssany was able to carry out these transactions as he was* *managing director of the Sorayanne Group, one of Iran's largest business conglomerates, and had personal ties with Khorasami, the president at the time, and officers from the Revolutionary Guards, who dominate Iran's business world. Zanssany became their front man. At the time of his arrest, he was worth around $13.5 billion.*

*However, this illicit revenue was earned during the period of time when Iran was under sanctions. The U.S. and the E.U. found out about the scheme and blacklisted Zanssany and his firms for helping Iran's government bypass international law. The Iranian government put all the blame on Zanssany, and detained him in Evin Prison in Tehran for financial crimes.*

*Zanssany was accused by the E.U. of being the key facilitator for Iran in the gas-for-gold scheme. They claimed he was the trader/broker. He was actually the front guy. Yet he denied the E.U.'s accusation, denied the gas-for-gold scheme ever existed, and called the Europeans' accusation against him a mistake.*

*Obviously a lie from Zanssany, and obviously he miscalculated his defense—he's in jail.*

*The Iranian government turned against him because they were caught trading and dealing in currency in the middle of international sanctions. Easier for the government to blame one greedy guy than to have the entire government blamed. In conclusion, the front guy became the fall guy for the Iranian government.*

*Zanssany claimed that the $2.7 billion he owes is in an escrow account for the Oil Ministry. However, the Central Bank of Iran cannot find the account. They're still looking for the money.*

*President Rustany has said that his government is fighting financial corruption, particularly with privileged figures. Meaning Zanssany, their proxy turned prey. Rustany doesn't want it made official that any part of the Iranian government is trading illegally or backing an illegal trader. Rustany wants to show he's obeying sanctions and is trustworthy, so he can nego-tiate a good treaty with the Americans to release funds. The Americans are holding $120-$160 billion for Iran in frozen assets.*

*Let's return to the dates to corroborate facts. Please look at the screen for these:*

- *December 17, 2013-* a group detained and questioned in Istanbul for the gas-for-gold scheme. This was at the time of the plane's "fog of war." Iranian Zanssany—who was aboard the plane, and had the cargo registered to his company, was one of the young men detained in Istanbul.
- *December 30, 2013 –* Thirteen days later, Zanssany was transferred to Tehran and jailed in Evin Prison.
- *March 6, 2016 –* More than three years later, Zanssany is still in jail, and on this day he is formally sentenced to death for embezzlement and spreading corruption on earth. That's the most serious crime in Iran. He will be killed by being hanged if he is found guilty.
- *March 19, 2016 –* Thirteen days later, Sharatt enters Miami airport with his family to visit Disney World.

Sharatt needed a vacation in Miami. Most likely, Sharatt feared he'd become the next fall guy—be it for Iran or Turkey.

Sharatt is Zanssany's best friend.

Cristina turned off the phone. "The transmission is finished for the day, my dear friend."

"It's like a chess game," Marina said. "Who will move next?"

"This is so interesting, and it's even more interesting to be able to share it with you," Cristina commented.

"I think your husband's investigative work has rubbed off on you. Be careful—detective work always involves danger." They both laughed.

Cristina took her phone off the bracket and turned the radio to a classical music channel. She smiled, listening to Mozart's *Elvira Madigan's Piano Concerto,* and hummed along. "Lovely," she said to the tune of the piano's theme.

Then Cristina paused and addressed her friend. "Tell me, *ma chère,* what did you do yesterday without me? Did you miss me? Maybe not; you look very happy. Is that a glow to your skin I detect?"

"Well, I met a very interesting man." Marina winked at her friend.

"Don't tell me that a man popped out of a mesquite bush with a bow and arrow and pierced your heart with an arrow?"

"No, he had a revolver at his hip."

"How sexy! Tell me more."

"Actually, you'll meet him shortly, at the Taos pueblo."

"He lives in the *pueblo?*" Cristina's voice reflected her surprise.

"I didn't ask him where he lives. Maybe in the mountains or the desert. He seems to know a lot about them."

"Did you start searching for the treasure? He'd be a good guide."

"We're waiting for you, *ma chère.* The three of us, *ensemble.*"

"*Merci.*" And Cristina threw her a kiss. "So what did the two of you talk about?"

"Cacti, cat's claw, digitalis, coconut oil, and aloe."

"*Fascinant.* What an inspiring conversation."

"It was. He knows a lot about beauty and youth, from a different perspective."

"That's my friend—always searching for a treasure of information."

"Actually, he's quite a treasure. You'll see what I mean."

Cristina eyed her curiously. Marina had many beaus and admirers—a woman sought after by men. She was a striking figure: tall, voluptuous, chic, carrying herself with confidence and charm. Multiple magazine and news articles spoke of her success as a rags to riches story. They always mentioned how philanthropic she was, helping thousands of refugee children. But she hadn't given herself to a man since Stefan.

"There's the pueblo!" Marina announced with a great deal of pleasure in her voice. "His name is Tahquitz. We arranged to meet at the side entrance. There he is!" she called out, excited.

"Where?" Cristina asked, staring at a group of Tanoan Indians.

"The tall, thin guy. I think he's about 6'2", with the white Stetson hat and long silver hair."

Marina slowed down driving and opened the window. "Tahquitz!" she yelled.

He approached the car, smiled, took off his hat, and bowed. "Hi Marina, and good morning to you both. We have a beautiful day for a hike and a treasure hunt."

Cristina climbed into the back seat of the jeep so Tahquitz could sit next to Marina. "Please—it's easier to give directions from the front," she said diplomatically, sensing that Marina wanted to have him near.

"Sounds good to me," he replied, taking off his hat in respect to the women. "Best to start the hunt, according to Mr. Fenn, at the base of the Rio Pueblo. It's called that because a small river flows through the middle of the pueblo."

"Good idea," Marina agreed.

"I used to hike there as a boy. I remember it took three nights in the summer for me to reach the peak."

"I hope it won't take us that long," Marina joked.

"Not at all. Mr. Fenn specified twenty-four clues to where the treasure is located, and it seems the trail spreads in the lower parts of the mountain range. About four miles. Are you gals up to that?"

"Sure," Cristina answered. "We're dressed and equipped for anything." She tipped her straw hat with its Parisian, Dali design.

"Glad your spirit is prepared," he said, and laughed. "The Great Spirit will be happy with you both."

"Who or what is that?" Cristina asked, mystified. She had missed Tahquitz's explanation yesterday. This was all new to her.

"The Great Spirit is god-like. He rules over the Tanoan world, which is this desert and the mountains, and all the people, plants, and animals that are within it. The water spirit is his dearest follower. Water is the center of life in the desert because there's not much of it."

"Oh, don't worry about us," Marina assured him. "We filled up our canteens."

"You'll need more than water in the desert," he told her, laughing. "You also need patience. Part of the desert's mystical power is that it offers time to think and feel. The key is to listen to clues like winds whistling, birds in flight. They can tell you if nature will change. If day will turn dark in seconds."

"Well, I hope not today," Cristina commented.

"Don't worry, Tahquitz will protect us," Marina reassured Cristina, and smiled at her new friend.

---

They found the parking lot, and again theirs was the only car there. "Do we have a system?" Cristina asked while looking for her gear. "Do we trek from one clue to the next?"

"That's right," Tahquitz responded, checking the number of bullets in his gun. Cristina eyed Marina with a worried stare and hesitated to collect her gear.

"Don't worry," Marina repeated to her friend. "He's our bodyguard."

"We'll start at the northern lower ridge of the canyon," he pointed. "Fenn said in verse one, 'Look to the street.' He meant *calle,* the Spanish word for street. There we can find ancient dwellings built by my ancestors that were carved into canyons and limestone cliffs to create small houses. The stone dwellings were constructed in a long row, in front of a line of large boulders, which gave them protection from the wind, and followed a linear design, like a street. You can see it from here." He took his binoculars and passed them to the women.

"And the next clue?" Cristina asked, walking with Marina as Tahquitz led the way.

"Look to the right. There's an abandoned horse stable at the end of the canyon. Horses were our first trade with the Spanish. We gave them animal skins, and they exchanged the furs for horses. It changed our lives so we, Indians, could travel and explore."

Marina asked Tahquitz if he'd tell them about the plants as they hiked. "I'm so eager to learn from you," and she moved next to him, following his long-legged pace while Cristina lingered behind.

"The desert has lots of life," Tahquitz said. "That's why Mr. Fenn put his hunt in the desert. After recovering from cancer, he hiked there every day to gather strength. Each of the twenty-four clues are related to survival."

"So we've found clues one and two already," Cristina summarized. "First clue: caves for protection, and second clue: horses for exploring. Wait," she said, opening her backpack. "I have paper and pencil. I always travel prepared. I'll draw a map with the clues." She sat down on a rock and in several minutes finished the sketch and shared it with her friends.

"Lovely," Marina said. "My friend, the artist. Now for number three."

"Over there," Tahquitz said. "There's a large thicket of prickly pear cacti. Let me have your cell for a moment." Marina took it out of her backpack and gave it to him. He pressed the flashlight app and walked over to the grove. When the light touched several cacti, dozens of sharp spines appeared.

"When I was a child," he confessed, "I pretended I could live in the desert as a cactus, so the spines would protect me from harm."

Marina stared at Tahquitz. His words were simple and deep. She moved closer and whispered, "I hope no harm ever comes your way."

"Let me give you a gift for your goodness." He cut a piece from the cactus, stripped off the thorny skin, and handed her a piece of pulp. "Please taste this as my thanks."

"Tastes like watermelon—juicy and sweet."

"Can I try?" Cristina asked, and Tahquitz cut another piece for her.

"August," he told them, "is the first month of the Tanoan calendar because it's harvest month. The women gather berries from barrel cactus and boil it for a syrup. Tastes like lemon mixed with kiwi. It's our nectar."

"I remember that nectar was the favorite drink of the Greek gods," Marina said. He smiled at her, then lowered his eyes. She sensed he wanted to say something, but was shy.

"What's that plant?" Cristina interrupted the moment of awkwardness. "It's shaped like candles."

"*Cirios del Señor,* named by the Spaniards, candles of the Lord. It's a type of yucca," he said. "It has a white or purple flower and is known for its hardiness. It's New Mexico's official flower."

Cristina stepped backwards and looked upward to its tip.

"*Magnifique. Comme c'est beau.* In the sun, the top looks golden against the blue sky."

"Our fourth clue: Candles of the Lord."

"Let me draw it on my map." Cristina sat again on a rock to do her work. This time she saw an animal that looked like a mouse with a lizard in its mouth. She said nothing.

"What's that fragrance?" Marina asked.

"Desert mesquite."

"It smells sweet."

"That would make a good perfume," Tahquitz said. "The wood is used for campfires—it gives grilled meat a special taste."

"Is that clue number five?" Cristina asked.

"Sure is. Look at the dozens of mesquite bushes against the pile of desert rocks. That's the grove, according to Fenn. The Tanoans crush the seeds for baking bread. Makes it taste sweet like cake. When it's boiled, it's used for tea and helps you overcome sore throats, even bronchitis."

Marina picked up a fallen branch, rubbed the wood in her hand, and smelled her hands. "I don't recognize this scent. It hasn't been used before as a cologne or in a cream. It could also be used for a man. It's a rugged scent, yet tender. It evokes a sense of kindness."

Cristina did the same. "Maybe you've found your treasure."

"Treasure? Desert mesquite?" he asked, puzzled.

"Well," Marina said, thinking how, and if, she should explain a little about herself. She hesitated, but then continued. "You see, my work has some points in common with your world. I've become familiar with plants and herbs."

"Marina is being modest," Cristina interjected. "She's very successful in the field of cosmetics."

"Your work is beauty?" he asked.

"In a way, you could say that."

"Have you ever explored beauty from the inside?" Tahquitz

asked Marina. "That's a secret from the desert. Plants can make a person beautiful inside as well as outside."

"What do you mean?"

"The right plants can give you calm, vigor, and balance. People need all three to be happy. If they're happy with themselves, this pleasure is reflected on the face—from the inside to the outside of the person. It makes them look more beautiful."

"You're right!" Marina exclaimed. "Inside and outside; balance and equilibrium. A radiance from calm and vigor. What a great way to market beauty and plants!"

He smiled, pleased to see Marina happy. Tahquitz turned to Cristina. "Do you work with Marina?"

"No, Marina and I have been friends since school in Romania. I live in Paris with my husband, and I work in fashion and design. Marina isn't married, and she lives and works in New York City. But my work is related also to beauty. I use beautiful fabrics. They excite my imagination."

"I can understand that."

"But I think we've distracted you from our hike and the treasure hunt," Marina reminded him.

"No distraction. I'm very happy to hear about your world. The world here in New Mexico is so different."

"Wouldn't it be special to merge the plants of your world with the plants of my world to create a beauty that's little known?" Marina said. "We could create harmony and calm for the soul, but also offer *le dernier cri* of external beauty. What a goal!"

"Quite a challenge," he responded. "I don't know if you could package all those elements in a jar or put them in a cream. If you could ever manage it, you'd find the fountain of youth that so many explorers searched for. Perhaps the treasure you're chasing is just that: a fountain of youth, and this quest has brought you here. Fate. Destiny. And my good luck." He took off his hat and bowed to her.

Marina smiled at him. There was something about his words and his soulful way of expressing himself that touched her. She felt her entire body fill up with warmth. She hadn't felt this way in years.

———

They continued walking and talking. "We've got some animals for clues," Tahquitz announced, pointing to the ground. "Mr. Fenn likes them, too—they're survivors. Clue number six."

Marina and Cristina looked where he was pointing.

"Behind the rock, hiding. It's unusual to see this animal during the day."

"It looks like a mouse."

"It's a kangaroo rat. He can go an entire lifetime without a drink of water."

"A real survivor," Marina commented. "No wonder Mr. Fenn used him as a clue."

"It may look like a mouse and be called a rat, but it's actually related more to a gopher," Tahquitz explained. "Look how it eats."

The women studied its plump body and mouth and watched as it shuffled insects into its cheeks that looked like pouches.

"That's our clue—a survivor who drinks nothing yet eats well."

"No water? How's that possible?" Cristina asked as she sketched the animal.

"It has a secret. Look at the long nose tilting down to its mouth. The animal can capture moisture from its own breath as it exhales and then shift the moisture into his mouth. Though..." Tahquitz stopped talking. "Must be some trouble nearby," he said.

"Why do you say that?" Marina asked, looking around as she turned in a full circle. "Everything appears calm."

"The kangaroo rat is telling us the contrary. He's nocturnal. If we see him in daylight, it means there's danger. Something frightening forced him out of his safe rock."

Just as Tahquitz said those words, the kangaroo rat rushed away. A flock of roadrunners darted down and tried to capture him.

"That means something, too," Tahquitz commented. "Roadrunners usually walk. They only fly when they're afraid of a predator or other danger."

"I read somewhere that animals can feel danger before it actually happens. Birds at sea can detect a tsunami the day before..." Cristina didn't finish.

There was a gunshot. Marina and Cristina looked down at the sound and stared at Tahquitz.

"Don't be alarmed, ladies. Just a snake. And a venomous one at that. It was a bit too close to your leg, Marina—a very pretty leg. I couldn't let him bite you. I just scared him away."

Marina watched as the rattlesnake slithered away from them. "Why didn't you kill it?" she asked.

"There's no need. They aren't aggressive; we just frightened it. It needed some coaxing to leave. They're sensitive to vibrations, so I shot that log near it. The vibrations disturbed it, and it left."

Cristina jumped and whispered in fright, "I hate snakes! I really hate them."

The sky turned dark. "Do you think there's a storm coming?" Marina asked Tahquitz in a strange, calm voice. She knew she should be concerned—the rattlesnake and a storm—but somehow she wasn't. Perhaps it was because Tahquitz was near.

"We should head back," he said.

"What about our treasure hunt?" Marina asked, disappointed.

"You know, I read about this treasure hunt," Cristina said to her friend. "Mr. Fenn has had this going on for twenty years, and no one has ever found the treasure. Maybe it's like a placebo? It just makes you feel better, but it's not the real thing. I do feel better after this hike."

Marina laughed. "Anti-Machiavellian. The means justifies the end."

"I think we have maybe thirty minutes before the sky crackles in anger," Tahquitz warned.

"How do you know that?" Marina asked.

"See the flock of birds flying? Roadrunners again." He pointed to the mountains that appeared close, but far away. "Let's listen to nature. I don't want you to get soaked. We can take a shorter trail to where we left the car." He led them through a cactus grove over the rocks and above the boulders out of the mountain range.

As soon as they reached the red jeep, thunder rolled above them. Lightning streaked the black sky in white staccato flashes. The beauty of the desert quickly showed its harsher side.

"We just made it," Marina said as she helped Tahquitz put the canvas cover on the jeep.

"I feel mighty bad that your fun was spoiled," he apologized.

"Not your fault," Marina assured him as she put on the window wipers to the highest speed. "Maybe there's no treasure anyway. Just a thrill of the chase. That's what counts." She smiled at him so he wouldn't feel bad.

"I want to make it up to both of you," he stated and took her hand. He caressed her fingers in a way that made her entire body lose control—a thrill, excitement. She closed her eyes as his fingers lingered; she didn't want to move. She wanted more.

"Yes?" Cristina asked. "How?"

"If you're willing and have a week," he answered, "I know a place where fantasy is everywhere. We can resume our treasure hunt there."

"Another desert?"

"No—oceans and seas. Chimes that ring music. Underground caves that are hidden and lead nowhere. A mystery..." He smiled at

Marina. "You can find new herbs for beauty, and Cristina, you'll see fabrics more colorful than in your imagination."

"Sounds magical. Where is this place?"

"Istanbul. My sister has a home on the Bosphorus. Her husband is an important Turkish businessman. I started by spending holidays and summers with them, since I'm not married. I tend to spend more and more time there these days. I feel at home there, and have learned a bit of Turkish, too. I could show you around some of my favorite places."

He hesitated and looked down. Marina sensed his sadness.

"I lost my wife in childbirth—my child, too. I lost them both."

Marina closed her eyes. She felt sorry for him. They had a lot in common.

"We've never been to Turkey," Cristina said quickly, trying to change the mood. "What do you think, Marina? Can you get away? Summer is quiet for me in Paris."

"I don't know," Marina said. "I mean, this is all rather sudden. I like you, Tahquitz, but I don't know you all that well yet."

"Come on," Cristina said. "You'll be going with me. I'll protect you."

"Maybe," Marina said, sounding more convinced.

"How about July?" he asked.

Cristina yelped, "Yes!" while Marina shrugged.

"I guess so," Marina said.

"Can I phone you to discuss the details?" he asked.

"Of course. I'll give you my number," Marina said.

"Settled," he said, smiling. "Another treasure hunt. This one was just the beginning. It will be even better the second time around."

# 8

*New York City*
*March 31, 2017*

TAHQUITZ CALLED Marina the day after she returned to New York. He phoned early in the morning, hoping to get her at home before she left for work.

"Did I wake you?"

"No, I'm an early riser. I'm so happy you called."

"I keep thinking of you. I can't stop thinking of you," he confessed.

"Me, too." She placed her coffee and laptop aside and gave all her attention to the person on the phone.

"I'm already planning what to show you in Istanbul. Marina, I can't wait to see you."

"Me, too." She felt like a teenager. *But I'm not,* she reasoned. *Should I be the initiator? Or wait and let him?*

"Perhaps I can see you before? In New York? Or Santa Fe?"

"Do you know New York?"

"Not well."

"Then let me be your guide. And you can reciprocate in Istanbul."

"I don't want to impose on you. I'm sure you're busy. Work. Meetings."

"I want to see you too. When can you come?" She didn't want to hide her pleasure. Didn't want to play games. *The only way this will work*, she thought, *is to be honest.*

"How about next weekend?" He waited, allowing her to think.

"Yes. Friday? Thursday?"

"Friday."

"Please, don't book a hotel."

There—she said it, and then she wondered if she had been too forward or too aggressive.

---

He rang the doorbell, and she ran to answer it. He wasn't wearing his white Stetson hat, and his silvery hair was pulled tight back in a ponytail. He looked very distinguished in a double-breasted navy blazer and green tie that made his hazel eyes appear green. His skin had an outdoor, rustic tan. She felt uneasy thinking about how attractive he was.

He kissed her hello on both cheeks. She put her arm through his and led him into the living room. "Please come inside. You can leave your bag in the corner."

"What a beautiful view," he said, letting his eyes admire her silhouette rather than focusing on the view of Central Park. She was dressed in black slacks, black heels, and a red sweater with a low neckline that showed the curve of her breasts. "Everything is beautiful," he commented, admiring her attire.

She felt shy, noticing his stare. "Can I offer you something to eat or drink?"

"No, thanks. I'm fine."

"How about some wine? Will you join me in a glass?" She didn't want to tell him she needed some courage. "Red? White?"

"Whatever you like."

"This is a good one. To celebrate that you're here." She went to the bar in the corner of the room—a long marble counter in front of a wall lined with dozens and dozens of wine bottles. "Château Ausone St. Émilion, 1995." She handed him the bottle and smiled as if she were surrendering herself.

He stared into her dark eyes, "A special vintage." He opened it carefully, aware of the treasure she was offering.

She placed two wine glasses on the counter and took from the small fridge a sampling of cheeses. From the cabinet, she brought out a box of crackers and busied herself so as not to think. She breathed deeply; told herself not to reason. Not to hold back. To be free. Like she was eighteen again.

Tahquitz poured some wine into his glass, swished it a few times, and brought it to the remaining light of Central Park as the sun began to set. Colors of red reflected from the sky to mix with the ruby wine. He showed Marina. "Beauty to beauty," he said. "Nothing could be more wonderful." He poured her glass full.

They walked to the couch, sat down, and then nervously, Marina eyed the fireplace. She had started it a while ago, and now the fire needed care. She took the bellows leaning against the wall and concentrated on the glowing embers. She placed a long, thin branch on top of a beginning flame and squeezed the handle-bellows until the fire pierced through.

"I'm admiring how delicately you revived the flames."

"I haven't made a fire in a while. I thought it would make the room more inviting. I used to do it often in Transylvania."

"I hear it's very beautiful there."

"Yes. The Carpathian Mountains—very different from the Rockies and Taos. They'r very green—lined with peaks of evergreens."

He poured her some more wine. They chatted and laughed. She spoke of Transylvania when she was growing up, a place where it was cold, with no heat, no light, no life. But that was where she and her friends were from, Cristina, Mica, and Anca—the Four Musketeers. And together, they'd good times. They had given each other strength.

The fire soared. She walked over to it and repositioned the log to make it one with the flames. "It doesn't smell as sweet as mesquite." Nervous, she didn't know what else to say.

He went to her aamd took her in his arms, "Sweeter." He kissed her on the neck, on the cheeks, on her lips, long and hard. "I feel so much for you. A burning inside me. I want to be one with you, feel you close."

"I feel it, too."

He took the glass from her hand and placed her softly on the rug before the fire. He kissed her, raised her sweater, freed her. She allowed his kisses to cloud her mind and she to feel the wine. He caressed her stomach, her thighs. She closed her eyes. He removed her bra, kissed her breasts, her stomach, that whispered more. She unbuttoned his shirt, his pants. She stroked his body with her hands, her lips. The heat of passion burned inside. She was on fire. He took each breast in his palm and kissed the nipples until they were hard. He removed her slacks, underpants, stockings. Took her tightly in his arms, moved into her, entered deep with all his thirst. She lost herself in him. Her passion raised her higher and higher, deeper and deeper. She floated up, wanting to burst. Scream. Yell. Die. More and more.

He kissed her wet hair, soft and damp with pleasure. He drank in her passion as she moved beneath him. Their bodies burned as one, and in their fire, they forgot what they were doing, where they were, where they were going. There was no place, no time, no words. Everything stopped except their bodies moving tightly with each other until they were one.

For several minutes, Marina stayed in Tahquitz's arms without moving, feigning sleep. But despite her closed eyes, she was very much awake, savoring the pleasure he had just given her. Strong and soft, he had entered deeply into her. And he had entered into her soul. With her eyes shut tight, Marina tried to hold on to the moment.

They lay naked next to the fireplace. He covered her with his kisses. "You feel so warm," he said.

She laughed. "Not because of the logs on fire."

"The first time I saw you, I knew you were passionate."

"How did you know?"

"Your dark eyes, almost black, your lips so full and ripe, your laugh, so deep from your soul. I knew because you showed me. And I wanted to know you more."

"The only thing we need to know is that we're here together." She closed her eyes, wanting to go slowly.

"Marina, I will always be sensitive to you."

"I trust you. I feel your goodness."

He took her into his arms and held her close, soft and tender, strong and sure, without saying a word.

———

Tahquitz came every weekend to visit Marina. She relished showing him the city she loved. They toured neighborhoods of foreign stores, where they'd pretend to be in another country. Dim sum in Chinatown. Rigatoni in Little Italy. Kimchi in Korean town. Eclairs on the East side. Gelato on the West side. All the corners of the world in the city she knew—and all topped with kisses. The days ended at Marina's place where they chatted and laughed in front of the fireplace as the sunset covered Central Park in orange and red. They delighted at the city lights, lighting the end of day, appearing like a string of white pearls as they cuddled in each other's arms. Happy, they made love until day lost its light and night reminded them how content they were together.

Spring came to New York City with flowers and sun and the promise of new beginnings. During the week, Marina worked as hard as before, but with an added energy as she experimented with new plants and herbs. Tahquitz remained in Taos, where he had his work at the Indian reservation clinic as well as at the Tanoan Foundation, guiding students to continue their studies.

But on Fridays, Tahquitz came to New York and went directly to Marina's lab, where he'd work beside her. His studies in medicine and his knowledge of using plants for healing helped him understand the component parts of many of the plants and herbs she was experimenting with. It was easy and natural for him to advise her. And yet he did so unobtrusively, always mindful that the lab and research were under her tight supervision. He respected how she ran her experiments and interfaced with her assistants. And she appreciated his tact. Little by little, she deferred to him on practical matters, for she realized that she understood the chemical nature of the plants from an academic perspective, but he knew their practical use, which was ultimately the most important component of her research. They complemented each other and enjoyed the intellectual exchange of working together.

On weekends, they slept late, read the newspapers with breakfast, and settled in as a couple learning about each other. It was a time of renewal for both of them.

Tahquitz wanted to give so much to Marina, to please her and help her in any way possible. One morning, she complained about how frustrated she was with her computer. She kept getting messages about updating her software and apps, and she didn't know how to do it.

Tahquitz offered to help. "My hobby," he told her. "I love all electronic gadgets."

After he adjusted her computer, he asked if she had any problems with her phone and helped her install, update, delete, and block all the data she had neglected to do.

"I have another idea," he told her. "What if I duplicate and transfer your important documents from the office computer system to your home computer? In this way, you have the choice to work privately at home on some files."

He even showed her dozens of apps and programs he could install for her to enhance her research.

"What did I do before, without you?"

But what they liked to do the most on weekends was to stroll through New York City's outdoor green markets in search of herbs and plants they hadn't known before. It was as if they were continuing their treasure hunt, just like their first time in Taos, and the treasure was the discovery of each other.

## 9

*New York City*
*April 1, 2017*

IT WAS A RAINY, lazy Sunday in New York. Marina indulged in her favorite matinal ritual of espresso and the news of the day, while Tahquitz tinkered with her laptop. As he was transferring some files, he asked her, "What else can I do for you with this machine?"

"You're spoiling me."

"I hope so. I want to offer you the world. By improving your computer, I hope to do just that."

"You are special—an old-fashioned shaman and a modern techy." She smiled and hugged him.

"I know what else I can do for you. I can set up an alert on your phone. That way, you can get immediate information about whatever news item is happening as it comes in."

"Who knew? You're a magician also."

"All the more to please you, m'lady. Let me see your phone."

Marina went to the counter, unhooked it from its charger, and handed it to him.

"Who or what are you interested in?"

"Recep Sharatt."

Marina noticed that upon hearing the name, Tahquitz flinched. His body looked stiff and angry, but he didn't say anything. Marina found that odd. She sensed he wanted to tell her something, but she just let it drop, and instead focused on watching him work on her phone.

In less than a minute, he was finished. "Look," he showed her. "You already have a Google alert, and the name Sharatt has appeared with another name, a man called Mohamet Hakan Akan. Do you know anything about him?"

"Nope. Not a clue."

"Well, here's from an article from BBC News that explains," he said. He began to read to her:

F.B.I. agents arrested Mohamet Hakan Akan a few days ago, on March 27, 2017, upon his departure at J.F.K. International Airport in New York. Akan is the Deputy-C.E.O. of Hachebanque of Turkey, registered as Hache Bankasi, the official state-owned bank of the Turkish government.
Hachebanque is the conduit that facilitated the laundering of billions of dollars of gold in the gas-for-gold scheme between Turkey and Iran. The bank has liaised with eight International banks in New York City that are also involved with this scheme to help Iran circumvent sanctions.

"And here's a photo of Akan," Tahquitz said, showing the screen to Marina. "It also says there are tapes of phone conversations and text messages between Akan and Sharatt. The tapes confirm that they're working together."

Marina took the phone from him. "Let me finish reading it," she said. She scrolled to the next screen:

Akan has offered $50 million for bail, which has been denied by the American court. Judge Robert Friedman of the case explained that if the defendant were able to reach Turkish soil, the Turkish government would never give him back for trial.

"What does all that mean?" Tahquitz asked.

"I believe the real question is, why did Akan come to New York City, then leave the city once he was already safe? Was he trying to get arrested in New York? Or make a deal with the American government?"

She threw the phone on the counter. "Enough of this. Let's have another espresso or something."

Tahquitz and Marina settled onto the bench in the breakfast nook with fresh espresso and cranberry scones.

"Akan's going to need a top lawyer," Tahquitz said. He picked at the scone with his fork, rendering it a pile of crumbs.

"Ironically, the best criminal lawyer in town is already taken," Marina said. "His new client is Recep Sharatt. That lawyer doesn't like losing. His last client was a high-profile French politician, Dominique Cahan. Word came out that his wife had to give up a multi-million-dollar Impressionist painting to pay his legal fees and get her husband out of jail. He was the head of the Global Monetary Foundation at the time. He was also involved in a sex scandal with a hotel chambermaid in Manhattan."

"Wow, fun people," Tahquitz laughed. "How do you know all this inside baseball?"

Marina's laptop dinged with another alert.

"A vlog post from Finland," she said. "I've been getting transmissions once a week about this case, directly from Helsinki."

She turned the screen so they could both read:

Dear viewers from around the world, we wish to share with you a segment from the American White House taken by our prize-winning Finnish journalist, Tuula Komolin. She is sending both text and video. We'll alternate between each format on our screen.

First, her written report:

It was a beautiful spring day at the White House. American President Helmut Hoss was standing in front of the Rose Garden for a photo-op, smiling proudly, as if he himself had arranged the red roses to coordinate with his red tie and the red carpet leading to the White House for the man he was honoring next to him, President Riza Tarik Ozogant of Turkey.

The American president began by clapping for himself. Why, no one knew. He raised his arms waiting for cheers, but nothing came, so he continued talking. "America and Turkey. They tell me we're friends. I'm a fan of their president. Great guy. A strong man. Doing great things with me to make us both great!'"

Ozogant pouted and his thin mustache twisted slightly. He leaned toward the microphone and commented, "Turkey will not accept Kurds having power in Syria or Iraq. We'll bury them in ditches! The Kurds are terrorists who want…" His face turned red, and he did not finish his sentence. Instead, he began a discussion with the man next to him about Turkey's airbase, Incirlik. Located near Turkey's Syrian border, it hosts 1,500 U.S. troops and is being used for air strikes against ISIS by the Americans. The Turkish president threatened to close it. But until they negotiated, Ozogant didn't mention that Sharatt's holding company, Royal A.S., and his trading company, Zavirr Gold, had their offices in Hoss Tower Istanbul. The detail would just get the American president prickly.

Hoss appeared lost in his own thoughts. Turkey owed the U.S. $17 billion from unpaid loans. And there was a $100 billion deal on the table from Turkish companies. Hoss had told the press he wanted the deal.

*"Listeners,"* interrupted the narrator, *"we are switching our equipment to a live-streaming video. Fighting has just erupted outside the White House main gate!"*

The video feed showed Ozogant walking toward his security guard. A secret microphone picked up what the guard was saying to the Turkish president:

*"Two of our security agents, who were outside the Turkish Ambassador's residence, have been arrested and booked by the Washington D.C. police. Apparently, they beat up an American police officer. Video cameras filmed our guards throwing the officer to the ground and kicking him in the face. They also got on camera a*

*woman with an American flag who was beaten up by our agents and is bleeding."*

The narrator summarized: *"In all, nine American anti-Ozogant protestors have been wounded by Turkish agents and the victims taken to the hospital. There were protesters yelling and carrying placards stating, 'Remove Dictator Ozogant! Stop hostage arrests of the innocent in Turkey.'*

*"Viewers, please return to our text and read on."*

Marina sighed. "How can they get away with this? I mean, Turkish guards beating up Americans on American soil? It's unprecedented."

Tahquitz leaned in, shaking his head. "I guess that's what happens when you have a mutual admiration society between two goons."

They continued to read:

Ozogant has publicly scorned the idea of freedom of speech. After 2002, when his party won the elections, he publicly committed to less democracy in Turkey, not more.

In the past year, he has proven his point by arresting more than 100,000 people and shutting down dozens of newspapers, media channels, courts, and schools. Human rights are not a right, Ozogant has said, and no such right has a right to exist in his country.

According to an unnamed source inside the White House, there was an envelope marked URGENT on the president's chair in the Oval Office this morning, with General Ike Flemm's name printed on the corner.

Of course, we have no way to know what was in that envelope, but we have learned from other sources that the General allegedly 'forgot' to register as a lobbyist for Turkey. He also 'forgot' about a $530,000 check he received for a consulting fee. The White House is being subpoenaed for documents to remind the General.

Our inside sources also saw a note on the desk, which said:

URGENT NUMBER TWO. TO DISCUSS WITH OZOGANT AT LUNCH. ALONE. NO PRESS.

We can only speculate on the subject of this upcoming discussion, but there is rumor of a possible political prisoner swap between Recep Sharatt, who has been having problems with prisoners, and an American Evangelical Christian pastor, Anthony Barson from North Carolina, who led a church in Izmir for over twenty-three years.

Barson was arrested on October 7, 2016, accused of being a terrorist and spy and plotting to bring down Ozogant. His sentence consists of three years, one month, and fifteen days in prison. According to the F.B.I., this crime is a fabrication and the pastor is completely innocent—a victim of a hostage arrest, a system used often in Turkey. Public figures, like the pastor and even tourists, have been kidnapped and taken as hostages to be exchanged for Turkish nationals imprisoned in other countries.

Then the narrator interrupted again:

*Viewers, we are switching to the White House. Please watch our continuing live-stream, showing President Ozogant and President Hoss together.*

Ozogant entered the office, escorted by several Turkish security guards. Ozogant looked angry. The secret mic picked up the conversation again.

*"There has been an unnecessary arrest of my agents by your police! Your press took photos. This is embarrassing. I'm returning to Turkey!"* He moved to leave.

*"But Sultan... Don't you like that name?"* Hoss smacked him on the back. *"Sultan, I have an idea to discuss with you over lunch. Something that'll make you happy. Make us both smile in front of the press. Isn't that good diplomacy? A deal—a prisoner swap. Hostage diplomacy!'"*

Hoss slapped the Turkish president on the back again and gave a thumbs-up to a Turkish security guard. *"You see, we get along just swell. That's because we have more than 1,700 American companies in Turkey. They make billions for both of us every year."* Hoss put his hand on Ozogant's shoulder. *"I even spoke to several European leaders to bring up again your country's entry into the European Union. I'm your friend. I like tough guys."*

*"We don't trust the E.U.,"* Ozogant said. *"But I trust you to solve this pressing matter of our citizens, Sharatt and Akan, who have been in your prison far too long. I want them out—sooner rather than later. If I don't get what I want, I'll take your inaction as a plot against Turkey—a plot to bring us down financially."*

*"Financially?"* Hoss said. *"Well, yes, I am the expert at that.*

*Without me, the American stock market would crash. I'm the only one who can prop it up. I'm America's Chosen One."*

Ozogant stared at him in apparent disbelief. *"You, the Chosen One? How can that be? It's me! And the stock market? I'll put someone as head of the Turkish Boursa who we both know."*

Ozogant slammed the door and stormed out of the room.

The video went dark.

Marina heard her cell phone ring with another loud alert. "So much news coming in," she said. "Sorry."

She took her phone and saw a link to a transmission from Sweden. "My favorite podcast—*Crimes and Scandals,*" she told Tahquitz. "Two women in Sweden discuss international crimes. Their subject for the past few weeks has been this gas-for-gold case. I'm obsessed with it."

"I'm fascinated to see all this political interest coming from northern Europe," Tahquitz said.

"Are you really? This isn't boring you?"

"Well, we could take a break…"

"Just one more. Look at this."

*We'll give you this week's summary. Our government in Helsinki has hosted multiple conferences and treaties in our diplomatic role of arbitration. For this reason, our government has been nominated by a United Nations committee to investigate the gas-for-gold scandal that has violated international sanctions. We have received permission from this committee to make public and post the following posts and videos, in hope to illicit comments from our viewers, that could help in this investigation.*

*Here is the first report:*

Mr. Sharatt has financed Iran's Aire Homa,
the Iranian government's official
airlines. The airline has flown Iranian
military on planes without listing their
names with international security, and the
planes have ferried weapons to Hezbollah.
Our government is investigating this last
allocation—*who sold the arms?* Some say
it's Ozogant himself, but that's odd,
because Ozogant is theoretically against
Hezbollah. Remember, viewers, Hezbollah
are Shiites and Ozogant is a Sunni. Two
different denominations of Islam—and
rivals.

Also, we have learned that payments have
been made by Recep Sharatt and wired to
Bank Metall, an Iranian government-owned
bank, and Metall Exchange in Tehran, for
services related to a gas field in Iran.
The payments were made in the amount of
$3.7 billion on May 24, 2011. In addition,
one week later, on May 31, 2011, $30
million in U.S. currency was wired to
Metall Exchange in Tehran. And on November
11, 2013, $100 million was wired to Tehran
to the Iranian Ministry on behalf of
Sharatt.

*The next transmission involves President Ozogant, who wants his citizens, Sharatt and Akan, returned to Turkey immediately! President Hoss's press secretary has responded:*

*"If we grant these extraditions with Turkey, we need something in return. Something more than a hostage exchange. The American president has sent his personal lawyers to discuss such personal matters."*

*But, research for our program has shown that Mr. Scarpia has already received a $500,000 payment from Turkey. Is this from a deal that's a personal matter? Is he being paid for back channel politics? And why has his law firm asked him to resign?*

"Are we almost done?" Tahquitz asked. "I'm getting hungry."

"One more thing. There's a video—it's about Sharatt's wife. You know who she is, right?"

"Everyone knows who she is—not a bad singer. Not really my taste, but, I guess I'm in the minority on that."

"Yes, I forget how much you know about Turkey. Here, look at the video."

*Deniz Akar, the international superstar, filed for divorce in September 2016 after Sharrat's arrest. Recently, they have reconciled. He's in jail and she's living in their mansion on the Bosphorus with their daughter. He has three other mansions on the Bosphorus and sixteen other homes. His wife is quoted as saying that Recep promised to buy her the planet Mars and build another house there if she returns to him.*

*Our final communication for the week is of the highest importance. News has just started to circulate about the relationship of the Iranian past president and richest man in Iran, with Iranian-Turkish gold dealer, Recep Sharatt. To understand this friendship, we must ask these questions:*

*When and how did the former president Rafsanjani and Sharatt know each other? On what business deals did they conspire together? And why?*

*Our research will take us to explore more what is the relationship between these two men and their two countries, Iran and Turkey.*

"Can we please go to lunch now? That scone did nothing for me," Tahquitz said.

"Okay, okay. I know I'm a bit obsessive. Let's go," Marina answered, and gave him a peck on the cheek. "Where to?"

## 10

*Istanbul, Turkey*
*July 7, 2017*

TAHQUITZ GREETED Marina and Cristina at the front door. "I'm thrilled to see you in Istanbul, and slightly surprised you came. I hope the trip was easy."

"We met up at the airport, me coming from New York and Cristina from Paris."

Tahquitz took Marina in his arms and held her closely.

She felt a warmth fill her body.

"The new short hair is something," he told her.

"I just had it cut. I thought Turkey would be warmer than New York." For some unknown reason, she wanted to justify to herself why she had decided to wear it short after years of wearing her black hair shoulder length or in a chignon.

"I like it. It shows more of your beautiful face. Your dark eyes stand out even more."

Marina was embarrassed.

Cristina stepped in to cover her friend's discomfort. "In France, they say a woman who cuts her hair is looking to change her life."

"Will Turkey bring out a different side of you?" Tahquitz asked Marina.

She shrugged.

He smiled and then changed the subject. "I've planned so much for you both to see. Such wonders of lovely treasures in Turkey. Surprises await you." He took Marina's hand.

"My sister and brother-in-law had to go to Ankara for several days on business," he continued. "They apologize for not being here to greet you. Please leave your bags over there." He pointed to the hallway. "Aslan will take care of them. Let me offer you something refreshing to drink and eat." He pressed an intercom button on the wall and spoke in Turkish.

Marina remarked that Tahquitz looked and acted differently than in New York. He was more at ease in his Turkish surroundings, as if his persona became one with the culture, similar to the way he had become one with Santa Fe's desert and mountains. It didn't seem that New York was his city. *Maybe there is oo much of the superficial and not enough of the essential,* she thought.

"Let's go into the living room," he suggested. "The view is quite nice." He led them into a long rectangular room that had one wide horizontal window with sweeping views of the Bosphorus.

"Gorgeous!" Marina said. "Breathtaking! I didn't expect such a sight, and so many bridges."

"The real bridge is Istanbul, the city," Tahquitz replied proudly, "connecting two continents—Europe and Asia—a mosaic of Western and Asian civilizations."

"Tell me—what are we looking at in front of us?" Cristina asked, moving closer to the window.

"The Bosphorus Bridge is on the east, the Golden Horn waterway is on the west, on the southeast—Üsküdar, the Asian side of Turkey, and the Galatea Bridge in the center, which separates the two parts of the European side of Istanbul—Stamboul and Beyoglu, where we are."

"Looks like a Turner painting, with its sailboats, barges, steamers, and ferry boats amidst the fog," Cristina said.

"But Eastern," Marina added. "There are dozens of mosques with minarets. They just seem to soar vertically to the sky, all in harmony with the waterways. It reminds me of a swirling Dervish dancer."

Tahquitz laughed. "You did your research."

"I did. Just for fun."

"I'd say being with you is fun, especially your *élan vital*. Your love for life."

"I can't wait to see all of Turkey!" shouted Marina, to prove his remark.

"If you wish, after lunch, I can give you both a tour by motorboat. We can pass the Hagia Sophia and Topkapi Palace. I'd love to take you to Adalar, a group of islands in the Sea of Marmara. Just an hour's ride in my Chris Craft. We can stop at the island Büyükada, my favorite spot, and take a buggy ride. Then *chai* at the port and watch the sunset."

"Is it as beautiful as the sunsets in New York?" Marina asked.

"Beauty is beauty, and you can find beauty anywhere. But in Istanbul, the sunsets are accompanied by bells. The chimes come from the muezzins in the minarets, calling the devout to evening prayer. Everything turns to music and evokes a kaleidoscope of colors and cultures. I'm so thrilled to share it with you." His eyes lingered on Marina.

Aslan walked in with a tray of glasses in the shape of tulips. Marina eyed them curiously, and watched Aslan pour hot tea into the glasses.

"Apple chai," Tahquitz explained. "Wherever you go in Istanbul, to any store, any shop, they'll greet you with a hello and apple tea. They have a system in which they call a special number, give an order, and in one minute, a young boy appears with a tray and steaming tea in these special tulip glasses."

"Where do the boys come from?"

"A mystery."

Cristina sat down on one of the large cushions and caressed the fabric. "The gold thread is real, and the silk is of the finest quality," she commented.

"Yes," Tahquitz replied. "The silk panels on these walls come from the same shop. I made an appointment for you to visit the studio where they're made."

"Thanks so much," Cristina said, and she smiled.

He turned to Marina. "I'd love to take you to the mineral springs in Pamukkale, near Izmir, a day's ride from Istanbul. My friend has a laboratory there where he mixes special herbs and flowers to create some unique scents. They probably don't exist in the creams you're experimenting with."

"That would be great," Marina said. "It sounds like an adventure."

"I'd also love to show you the real secret of Istanbul—an underground city–comprised of hidden caves that can be as long as five miles underneath the floors of a café, restaurant, or store. These kinds of caves can be found below the Hagia Sophia and Topkapi. But best of all is the one below the Basilica Cistern–from the 4th century. It's the largest underground water well in the world. During the time of ancient Constantinople, it held something like 100,000 tons of water with water cascades and bridges. Today it's dry, but restored very dramatically with lights and footpaths to highlight the cistern's maze of several hundred caverns running below the city."

"I wouldn't want to fall into that," Cristina stated.

"You can swim, right?" Tahquitz joked. "But seriously, I want to take you to a carpet store owned by my friend. When he decorated it, he found the remains of a church below the wooden floors. It was from the first century and was dedicated to Mary. Most of the floor mosaics in the church are still intact, as well as several painted wall murals of Mary with her baby son.

"Across the street is a tobacco store that also has a small underground chapel with painted murals. All under the floor–hidden for 2,000 years."

"I hope they don't use it today for rifles and missile parts," Cristina said.

"You've been around Eugen too long," Marina laughed.

Cristina nodded and walked to the end of the picture window. "What's behind the tall fence next to your house?" she asked Tahquitz. "Looks like tight security, with all those pieces of broken glass cemented on top."

"Very tight. Seven years ago, a disreputable young man, about twenty-six years old then, bought it when he married Deniz Akar, Turkey's musical superstar. I never could understand why she married him. She's nine years older than he is, beautiful, charming, smart, and very successful."

"Are you talking about Sharatt?" Marina asked.

"Of course—your gold launderer and buddy, Recep. You remember the news reports. He's the one."

"No," Marina and Cristina said together. "Your neighbor? You never said anything about that."

"I keep trying to forget."

"Do you know him?" Marina asked, surprised. "Why didn't you tell me before, when I made you listen to all those news reports?"

"I wanted to hear what you thought about him, without my story being part of it." Tahquitz was growing angry. "He's a person who gives a bad name to other Turks. I'm sorry he's Turkish. I like Deniz. She's kind and talented, and her being involved with Sharatt has damaged her reputation. That's not right."

Marina was surprised at Tahquitz's display of anger—it was so unlike him. "But you acted like you barely knew what it was all about," Marina said. She was puzzled by his secrecy.

"In any event," Tahquitz said, "she lives alone with her six-year-old daughter. Now that her husband isn't there, my sister has become her close friend."

"Looks they have a large yacht, a plane, and two helicopters. Even a heliport, from what I can see," Cristina said.

"My sister was very annoyed with the coming and going of his helicopters. Day after day, all the time, with several young men going in and out. I'm glad he's not here." Tahquitz stopped talking.

"In any event, " he said. "Deniz is giving a concert tonight. We're invited. Want to go?"

"How can we say no?" Marina quickly replied. She couldn't believe she'd meet Recep's wife, or ex, or go to his house. "But wait, I thought you said her music wasn't your taste?"

"I was talking more about her taste in men, I think. So, I guess we're going." He quickly changed the conversation. "But, let's get out and about in Istanbul."

---

It was a beautiful sunset from Büyükada. Cristina left their table at the port café to visit some shops she had admired. Marina and Tahquitz were alone, sipping apple chai as the last rays of red colored the sea and sky. Tahquitz seemed quiet after his outburst of emotion when talking about Recep Sharatt and was staring at the beauty surrounding them.

"I'm glad I can share with you the Istanbul I love," he said, taking her hand.

"I feel very privileged—a private tour, your boat, your…"

"Büyükada is special for me. I come here often at the end of the day to watch the sunset from this café. Not much has changed on this island in a hundred years. I like that."

"Looks like time has stopped. No cars. No rushing. Worries are left behind in Istanbul."

He remained quiet. She noticed he was breathing deeply, hesitating to speak, as if he was trying to phrase what to say next. He kissed the palm of her hand and caressed her ring finger. "You have long fingers. Lovely." It seemed he wanted to say something more—perhaps to ask if a wedding ring had ever been on one of her fingers—but he hesitated. "We've been so close these three months. Yet I feel I'm blocked. I wish you could talk to me, share with me what's inside you," he said.

She took her hand away to free herself from his questions. She closed her eyes as a way to say no.

"When I first met you," he said, "I told you I had lost my wife in childbirth." He took a deep breath and stopped talking. Marina moved closer and encouraged him to continue.

"I met Tala in medical school in Denver. She was also a Native American from the Chickasaw tribe in Oklahoma. We had a lot in common. Of the thousands of medical students that graduated in the United States in our year, only 30 were Indians. We were both lucky that we could concentrate on our studies and not worry about tuition or expenses. My grandfather's foundation paid for my studies—and he encouraged me to become a doctor. It was his dream that I continue his work and help our tribe. Tala's people, the Chickasaws, also had a great deal of wealth from their land which was rich in oil, gas, sulphur, and business ventures—casinos. They had a highly endowed scholarship fund and were thrilled to support Tala—their jewel." Tahquitz stopped talking.

"If this is too difficult…," she began.

"No. I want to tell you. It's here in Istanbul, not New York, that I feel freer to talk about myself."

He took a deep breath and continued. "After we married, we stayed at the University of Colorado for our internship and residency. I was in pediatrics and Tala was in surgery. She loved surgery. Said it was like a puzzle to fix the broken parts and make the body work again. Tala claimed it was giving a second chance to the patient to appreciate life."

He stopped talking again, put Marina's hand in her lap, and stood up. He said he was looking for the waiter. "Would you like another tea?" She sensed how difficult it was for him to talk about his past—as it was for her.

Tahquitz sat down, waved to the waiter, and asked for a plate of kebabs with two more teas. He continued talking.

"It was a good time. We had medicine and each other. In our second year of residency, Tala got pregnant. We were thrilled. It had been difficult for her. And then, the pregnancy was hard. Delivery..." He stopped again.

The waiter placed the beef kebabs on their table. Marina ordered a glass of mineral water. She noticed Tahquitz looked pale. His cheek bones appeared more sculpted than usual as the lower part of his face looked drawn.

Marina whispered, "I understand."

"I knew you would," was all he could say, and then after a few seconds, he whispered, "After some time of mourning, I returned to the tribe to fulfill my grandfather's wishes. I wanted to make a difference in our people's lives. I concentrated on the medical aspect. First I built a clinic for children with a pediatric emergency room. Then I added a daycare section and a small school to educate the mothers so they could learn a trade and work. As the children grew up, I made sure to know each one and encouraged them to go on to college. The tribe had the scholarship fund, and I became a mentor. The children needed help to continue their studies. They became my children."

Marina was moved by his story. Without realizing it, tears had welled in her eyes. Tahquitz had stopped talking. He looked down. She felt as if her heart was breaking for him.

"We have something in common." She wanted to tell him about

her philanthropy work with children, but she didn't want to sound as if she were competing with him. Instead she asked him, "Did you ever have someone you love die of cancer?"

He shook his head no.

"I lost the person I loved," she began. "Stefan and I were working together in Bucharest, in a lab, experimenting with plants, herbs, and all kinds of roots. Stefan had just received his Ph.D. in botany from the University of Cluj in Transylvania. He was the researcher for our team."

She paused. It was still painful. He took her hand.

"It was at that time that my childhood friend Mica was living in New York and had found a way to 'buy' Cristina and me so we could leave Romania."

"Buy?" he asked, surprised. "In a communist country?"

"Yes. The dictator Ceausescu was getting millions in cash to sell Romanian Jews and ethnic-German Romanians. Mica was in New York, had made a considerable amount of money, and knew Cristina and I wanted to get out. We were ethnic-German Romanians. Her lawyers arranged everything. Cristina went to Paris to work in fashion and I to New York City, to continue my plant experiments."

"And Stefan?"

"Stefan remained in Romania for a year while I was in New York, arranging with Mica's lawyers to get him out. But at that time, Ceausescu stopped his business dealings with Jews and Germans. The United Nations condemned him for acts against humanity—selling people. So Mica's lawyers had to find another way out for Stefan. And they did." She paused, took a deep breath. "But it wasn't an easy way out." She couldn't talk about that.

"When he got to New York, we married and worked together. Stefan was a true scientist. He was the one who discovered our first beauty creams. I did the publicity and marketing. Mica became our financial backer. We opened the first spa in the city.

New Yorkers love anything different. We marketed it as a way for women to feel beautiful." She nodded her head and bit her lip, remembering.

"Sounds like you and Stefan made a good team."

"Yes, for ten years—until he got sick." She stopped talking, drank some water, and paused. She closed her eyes and took a deep breath.

"Stefan smoked a lot. He couldn't stop. He tried so many times." Marina wiped tears from her cheeks. Tahquitz put his arm around her shoulder and brought her close to his chest.

"I set up a room for him in our apartment. After several months, it looked like a dark cave—foggy with special machines to help him breathe. He kept the lights off, windows closed, door shut. At the end, he allowed only the doctor and nurse to enter. He didn't want me to see him." Marina started to sob. "I couldn't save him. I tried so hard."

Tahquitz put his arms around her and held her tight. She felt his strength and understanding. After several minutes, she felt calmer. "I'm sorry. I didn't think I'd get so emotional. I haven't spoken about Stefan to anyone but my closest friends."

"I want to be close to you."

*Yes*, she wanted to answer, but something stopped her. Was she feeling guilty for having so many feelings for Tahquitz? *No*, she thought. *It's been more than twenty years. I have the right to love again. I should love again.*

She saw in front of her the faces of other boyfriends from her past, but whose relationships were less emotional than what she shared with Tahquitz, less soulful. They had been business associates. She had rationalized to herself that she needed a chaperone for her professional life. But Tahquitz was different–his *joie de vivre* was contagious. She felt excited with him, as if she were intoxicated, emotional with little control. Tahquitz was exciting and intelligent, sensitive and strong, with deep moral values. He had learned from his unusual life how to understand people's sufferings. It was natural for him to make her feel happy. And she wanted that.

She took his hand with the intention of explaining her thoughts when she heard chimes from the surrounding mosques. The sky was darkening, but a few lights from the harbor brightened the island. Men were preparing for evening prayer.

"In Turkey," he said, "the chimes call for renewal and indicate a new beginning." He held her tight in his arms and kissed her neck and cheeks softly, whispering, "I love you so much. Let me love you. Don't be afraid."

## 11

*Istanbul, Turkey*
*July 7, 2017*

THEY WALKED to Deniz's house, using her front entrance to show their invitation and pass through security. Marina and Cristina waited patiently in line while Tahquitz greeted several friends. Many languages were being exchanged among the international jet set. Cristina studied each person's style of dress—their hats, scarves, jewelry—knowing she'd store them in her memory until she could be back at her drawing board in Paris. She was tempted to take out her phone and photograph each person and their exotic clothing, but she noticed the security guards were insisting on collecting everyone's phone and storing them in a closet.

After passing through security, the three friends entered a living room, grander and larger than Tahquitz's sister's, with antique European furniture mixed with oriental carpets and large colorful silk cushions scattered on the floor. A young boy approached them with a tray of dates and apricots, and indicated that they should proceed to the dining room where there was a large buffet table filled with Turkish delights.

There were dozens of mezze—small appetizers—of *börekler* —feta cheese and meat-filled pastries in cigar shapes, as well as yogurts of white and pink, even some with tropical fruit. Thin wooden sticks of kebabs colored the table, consisting of red mullet and sword fish with alternating cubes of red and yellow tomatoes, onions and green peppers as well as kebabs of marinated beef, lamb, and mutton. Desserts decorated the setting with *lokumi*—soft jelly squares in flavors of rosewater, jasmine, and pistachio. There were dozens of squares of baklava with layers of pastry, honey, and shaved walnuts. Marble and chocolate halvah and honey-filled *kadayif* offered a choice of more sweets. Red and pink tulips were placed all around the room, and next to them were carafes of mineral water with orange peels floating inside. The dining room, so colorful and varied, gave pleasure to all senses, worthy of a feast for a sultan and his harem.

The three friends filled their plates and strolled around the room. Tahquitz was busy chatting with multiple guests, people who approached him with handshakes and hugs. He spoke Turkish with ease, and even spoke like a Turk with his hands as his body language reflected the atmosphere. Marina remembered he had told her that he had visited his sister and her husband multiple times since he was a teenager and learned the language because it reminded him of an Indian dialect.

Marina and Cristina entered a gallery that looked like a museum.

"Do you think this pastel is an original Renoir?"

Cristina nodded. "A forger could never achieve that pinkish-red tone on the cheeks like Renoir did. He made his own colors. Look at the texture of the skin. It looks so true." The artist in Cristina knew about hues.

"Is that one an original Van Gogh lithograph? The Potato Eaters? The number is low–6/9."

"Yes, that's authentic," asserted Cristina. "Follow the brush strokes next to the lantern, the only source of light. You can feel Van Gogh's sadness. A forger would just paint thick strokes minus the emotion."

"You like them?" Tahquitz asked as he approached them.

"How could you not?" Cristina commented. "Is this from her wealth or her husband's?"

"Her husband's and his dirty deals." Tahquitz took a deep breath and tried not to let the thought of Recep get him angry again. "I'm not sure if they're still married or if she's divorcing him. They periodically reconcile."

"If she's divorcing, I'd say it would pay for her to fight," Marina, ever the businesswoman, calculated.

"I can't believe I'm actually in his house!" Cristina said.

"*One* of his houses," Tahquitz corrected her.

"Now that we know you know him, do you know who he laundered the gold for?" Marina asked, smiling in a teasing way. She didn't want Tahquitz to be annoyed at the subject or her interest.

"That's the question," he replied, now in a calmer mood. "The Taoan Indians have a saying: Three things must come out: the sun, the moon, and the truth."

"Probably Eugen and Petre are searching for the truth," Marina said to Cristina, who then commented, "I guess the lawyers in New York are also."

"Do you think Recep's wife knows whose gold it is or was?" Marina asked Tahquitz.

"You'll meet her after the concert," he said, shrugging. "Maybe she'll slip some clues. For now, let's go outside to the garden and enjoy her singing."

As they followed the guests to the lawn, Marina noticed the

shrubs were cut into tulip shapes. "Will the concert be typically Turkish?" she asked him.

"Nope. I've heard she's into experimentation. And look at the TV cameras. She needs good press. Deserves it, too."

"I guess the right PR could sway a judge in her favor if she files for a divorce," Cristina commented.

"Hard to say," Tahquitz considered. "Judges in Turkey today are told what to say, or they land in jail along with hundreds of dissatisfied demonstrators."

"I hope a demonstration won't be on our tourist list," Cristina stated.

"Let's hope not. For now, let's grab those seats next to the xylophone."

"I love percussion instruments," Marina commented. "I remember as a kid, my favorite type of music was clapping hands and stomping my feet."

"Taoan Indians did the same thing a long time ago. Stomped their feet that had bells tied around their ankles. And rubbed stones and sticks to make a rhythm."

"I read that Turks in the old days used tulip glasses filled with different levels of water and tapped sticks on the glasses," Cristina said.

"Looks like that's the idea for tonight," Marina commented, noticing a table with six half-filled wine bottles next to the xylophone.

Their chatter was interrupted as Deniz Akar walked into the middle of the manicured green lawn. She smiled and turned to the Bosphorus behind her, bowed in deep respect to her city's waterway, and pointed to it, indicating that the lights and boats would serve as her backstage.

She took the microphone and welcomed her guests in different languages: *"Bon soir. Buona sera, guten abend, iyi aksamlar, good evening. So glad to see you all."* She continued in English. "I'll use the international language so all my friends will understand."

She moved closer to her seated guests and introduced the show.

"During the Ottoman Empire in Turkey, all forms of art such as mosaics, carpets, glass, and music, reproduced the mystery of the Orient. European musicians like Mozart used percussion instruments to evoke beautiful Turkey. His comic opera *The Abduction from the Seraglio* is set in a Turkish pasha's palace, and in the Overture, Mozart uses instruments not found in his other works, like the timpani, cymbals, triangle, and kettle drum. And in his violin concerto, which he entitled *Turkish* he recreates Dervish dancing. Mozart wanted music to be fun; to give pleasure and make people laugh.

"Tonight, I want you to have this same joy of listening to music that uses ancient percussion techniques in a modern way. I will accompany the musicians as if my voice was another instrument. I hope you enjoy."

Two handsome young men appeared next to her and bowed to the crowd. Each one was wearing a red fez with a black tassel and a red silk jacket with matching loose-fitting, black harem-style pants. The first musician moved to a table with six corked wine bottles filled with varying levels of liquid. He picked up a pair of sticks with square cloth-covered tips and began by tapping each bottle. He patted several times on the same bottle to introduce a melody.

The xylophone player picked up the tune by answering to the bottles in a responsive duet. Each musician played fragments that blended into the other's music and intermingled to form varying tones. Together, they alternated their melody as if they were children playing and sharing their fun. The audience laughed, some clapped, others yelled, *Bravo!*

Deniz joined the musicians on the grass lawn with the lights from two continents illuminating her petite, 5'3" frame. Draped with silk scarves on her upper and lower body, with golden bracelets at her wrists, she raised her microphone and sang in Turkish. Her sweet soprano timbre mixed with the musicians as they alternated their playing with each other. Tap, tap from the wine bottles. Clink, ring from the xylophones. Then came a response from the human voice as an echoing reply. Mysterious sounds blended as one.

The audience clapped and, transfixed, yelled, *"Encore!"*

"Of course," said Deniz, smiling. "I'm so glad you're enjoying it."

The musicians played on, each one in turn, responding to the other's melody, varying the themes in a dramatic reply to Deniz's voice, just wanting to give pleasure to everyone.

# 12

AT THE END of the concert, Deniz floated her dainty body through the garden like an angel, greeting her guests and accepting their praise. Graciously, she thanked each one. Then she saw Tahquitz, waved to him, and approached him for a cheek-to-cheek kiss.

"I'm so glad you came tonight. Did you enjoy the music? It wasn't too different from my usual, was it?"

"I loved it. You were wonderful."

"I was going to pass by your sister's house to see if you were there. I'm having problems with my computer. I don't know if I have to update some apps or maybe there's a virus. Or something else."

"I hope no one is spying on you," he said, concerned. "I'll stop by tomorrow."

Deniz nodded, appearing in control despite his warning, and turned to the ladies. "Tahquitz is a wizard with computers. Anything technical."

"Please," he said, "you're giving away all my secrets."

Deniz smiled. "When will we resume our backgammon tournament? Several guests tonight told me they're eager to start again now that you're here for the summer." She told the women, "He's also a wiz at backgammon. All of Turkey's officials want to play with him." Then she laughed. "I'm thinking of Tahquitz playing backgammon with Cemele Bertegon, Turkey's chief architect. When they start, they go on for hours."

Tahquitz nodded his head and smiled. "Cemele claims I'm lucky in dice. I prefer to be lucky in love. But let me introduce you to my friends, Marina Johannas and Cristina Patrisse. They're been friends since school days in Romania."

Deniz smiled warmly and shook their hands.

"I enjoyed your concert so much," Marina said. "You truly evoked the beauty and mystery of Turkey, combining the music with the Bosphorus as a backdrop for the stage. I noticed how you used the lights from the boats and land."

"Marvelous," echoed Cristina, extending her hand to her hostess. "I love the way your voice echoed the percussion instruments. It was an honor to hear you!"

"Thank you. I hope the TV station will do well financially. I organized the show as a charity for Turkish children who don't have enough money for food. So many of their parents have been arrested." She looked down. "Our government is afraid they'll lose control over the people, so they arrest anyone who doesn't agree with them."

Tahquitz shook his head sadly, but he didn't want to talk politics and decided to turn the conversation to something else. "Marina lives in New York City and Cristina lives in Paris."

"Oh," Deniz paused. "New York? Recep is there. We divorced and then reconciled and then…" She paused again. "Unfortunately, as you probably know, he's in Manhattan not as a tourist but as a prisoner." Her voice turned sad, and her body tightened.

Cristina and Marina moved closer.

"Still, I can't forgive him for what he did to me and our daughter. For such a brilliant man, he committed a crime against his family. Imagine at the Miami airport—four policemen arrested us. Astara is still traumatized." Deniz was aware that she was becoming emotional. "I'm sorry," she said. "I'm talking too much. I have that habit."

"It's odd," Cristina pursued. "Why would he come to the U.S— to risk getting arrested?"

"Not to mention to risk getting me and Astara arrested with him. They held us for hours, until I was able to call my New York media consultant for a lawyer." She stopped talking and looked around and whispered, "There was a good reason he went to Miami, and it wasn't for marlin fishing."

Deniz looked like she was trying not to lose her composure. Guests were staring at her. She motioned for them to follow her over to a tree, and she whispered, "He didn't trust Ozogant. Recep tried to keep him happy—gave him a 10% commission of all the profits. You know the word *baksheesh*, right? It is a Turkish word. How do you think Ozogant was able to build such a huge palace? But Recep wanted to stop. And they wouldn't let him stop. They even threatened to kill him."

Marina was surprised that Deniz was so open about what was happening. "Are you implying that he *wanted* to get arrested?" Marina asked. "Was it in order to make direct contact with the American government? Or trade his information for freedom?"

"Actually, he wants to end his life of crime," Deniz answered. "He told me so. I stopped our divorce proceedings because I believed him. But Ozogant wants more money, and Recep is his number one provider."

"What do you mean?" Marina couldn't keep from asking questions, as long as Deniz was willing to keep talking. "What is Recep doing for Ozogant?"

Deniz walked even farther away, to the side of the lawn where no one was around. She indicated that her listeners should follow her again. "Recep is the liaison between Iran and Turkey. His link is Rafsanjani. You know him, right?"

Both women nodded, yet they hesitated to say anything. They just stared at her, and Marina thought, what a small world—Rafsanjani and Ceausescu. Gold from Romania. Tahquitz being Recep's neighbor. Tahquitz is angry, living next door to Recep and sees how the gold is illegal and causes harm.

Deniz continued. She seemed worked up, perhaps from the emotion of singing before or from talking about Recep. Whatever it was, it seemed she needed to talk, and her listeners were avid to listen.

"Tahquitz said that you're friends from back in Romania. You probably know that Ceausescu, your beloved leader, had a very trusted friend—the richest man in Iran. Rafsanjani: president, imam, businessman, mentor."

"Well," answered Marina, "we actually do know something about Rafsanjani, but please, tell us more."

Deniz walked a little closer to the river and gestured for them to follow. In a lower voice, she explained. "Ceausescu went to Tehran sometime in December, 1989, to visit Rafsanjani, who was just elected president and had created a private bank—the Bank of Tehran. Ceausescu brought with him trunk-loads of gold bullion bars valued at $1 billion dollars for safekeeping in the new bank. He didn't trust the Swiss banks' secrecy laws. He trusted Iran more, given that the prior year, Romania and Iran's trade amounted to something like two billion dollars."

"Yes," interrupted Marina. "I remember Switzerland was revising their secrecy laws. They had opened up multiple accounts of political leaders who had been indicted and were being investigated, including Marcos in the Philippines."

"Oh, yeah," Cristina said. "I remember that case."

"Ceausescu stayed in Tehran for a couple days to confer about trade issues, and some private issues as well. His gold, no doubt," Deniz continued.

"Rafsanjani swore on the Koran to keep Ceausescu's gold a secret. To seal his loyalty, he supplied Ceausescu with Iranian *Pasdaran*—Revolutionary guards—to protect the dictator when he returned home."

"Yes, documented history," Cristina confirmed. "A bloody revolution."

"But there's more to the story," Deniz said. "A history of Ceausescu and Gaddafi—Libya's leader. They had been business partners since the 1970s."

"I remember Ceausescu's trial, "Marina said, "when the judge talked about Ceausescu's criminal partnership with Gaddafi. He accused the dictator of getting Romania involved in nuclear research sites, chemical and bacteriological warfare, terrorist training cells, and converting uranium to nuclear weapons."

Cristina shook her head in disgust. "They joined forces to satisfy their diabolic goals: Gaddafi wanted to be the leader of the Arab world, and Ceausescu wanted to be the richest man in Eastern Europe. They swore on the Koran in Tripoli that they'd be brothers forever."

"If I remember, Gaddafi sealed his friendship by giving Ceausescu a gift of two oil refineries in Libya," Marina said. "Ceausescu transported the raw oil by Romanian tankers and processed it in Romania into refined petrol. He claimed it was Romanian, to circumvent Libya's embargo, and he shipped the oil all over the world to increase his personal fortune."

"You remember correctly," Cristina confirmed. "Ceausescu got extremely rich from Gaddafi and their crimes, and insisted on being paid in gold.

"But also, and I want to emphasize, *also,*" she said in a determined voice, "our leader not only wanted to hide his gold in Iran, but also wanted to use a billion dollars to jump start a new international bank with Rafsanjani and Gaddafi. The idea was that this bank would lend money to poor countries at a low rate of interest."

"Did they ever form the bank?" Tahquitz asked.

"No, Ceausescu had to return quickly to squash the revolution, and he didn't have time to implement his plans. He was killed a few days later."

"And his gold in Tehran," Deniz said, "was never found or claimed. Rafsanjani continued to be President until 1997, and after that, he became the richest businessman in Iran, owning huge tracts of pistachio farms—Iran's leading export—as well as high tech start-ups, even an airline."

The women stood in uncomfortable silence.

"It's odd to think how close we all are to this history. It's not just an abstraction. It's our story."

"So true. And, fast forward fifteen years to 2011," Deniz continued. "An older and frailer Rafsanjani wants to get Ceausescu's gold out of Iran because he's under suspicion. He's too rich in a country that's suffering because of sanctions and trade embargoes. Rafsanjani realizes that the economy needs to be propped up or the Revolutionary Guard will use him as a scapegoat and kill him. His opponents claim he's working with the capitalistic West."

"If I recall," Cristina said, "Rafsanjani contacted his old friend Ozogant next. Ozogant is now Prime Minister of Turkey, of course, and is planning his campaign for a 2013 Presidency. Rafsanjani and Ozogant come up with a scheme to get the gold out of Iran to Turkey. A gas-for-gold scheme."

Deniz nodded, looking eager to add to the story. "They think of helicopters with firefighting buckets to carry heavy material—the gold—and they hide the gold inside the buckets, covered by food, medicine, and firefighting equipment. They also design special fire extinguishers inside which they can hide one gold bullion bar. They claim that they're using these goods for humanitarian reasons–their legal loophole–to fight fires. Ozogant remembers that his son, Belcan, has a good friend who is a licensed helicopter pilot."

"Recep!" Marina and Cristina exclaimed together.

"But before we talk further, let me show you something," Deniz said

Deniz walked across the lawn her house with her guests following. They proceeded into the living room. Her three eager listeners were silent. She went to her desk, an old fashioned Turkish antique whose top half opened up like a large book. She withdrew a key from her pocket, unlocked a drawer, and took out a magazine. She flashed the red cover, *Time*, and showed them a photo of Rafsanjani on the cover.

She handed it to them, and Cristina read the caption.

**RAFSANJANI. *The Return of Rafsanjani... Can He Be Trusted?***

"Wait, didn't he die in late 2017?" Marina asked, remembering how she had read about it in the *Times* before she went to Paris for Cristina's fashion show.

"Yes," Deniz said, "In September. But in 2013, Rafsanjani was at the peak of his activities. He was the man behind the present president, Rustany, and also Katammy, the Iranian president from 1997-2005."

"Rafsanjani was also the most influential Arab in the Islamic world in the 1990's," Marina stated in a voice that obliged attention.

Deniz stared at Marina. They all waited for her explanation.

"I remember my father told me the story about the Oslo Accords and how Yitzhak Rabin, the Israeli Prime Minister, and Yasser Arafat, the leader of the PLO, signed an agreement with President Clinton on the White House lawn in 1993. There was such hope for peace then. But the next day, Rafsanjani twisted any possible achievements by accusing Arafat of committing treason against the Palestinian people."

"Treason?"

"That was Rafsanjani's subterfuge. The truth was that if the Oslo Accords were successful, and the Arabs made peace with Israel, then Iran would be left isolated. There'd be a new Arab-Israeli alliance, without Iran being included or considered important. And as Rafsanjani feared, the Oslo Accords did help Israel establish diplomatic relations with several Arab states."

"So what happened?"

"Rabin was assassinated in 1995 at a rally in Tel Aviv while he was supporting the Oslo Accords. The assassin was an Israeli ultra-nationalist who opposed Rabin's peace results."

"I remember that," Tahquitz said. "A tragedy. I remember a few years later there was the Camp David summit to reaffirm the Oslo Accords, hosted again by President Clinton, but without any peace treaty."

"Yes," agreed Marina. "Rafsanjani worked hard to destroy peace in the Middle East, so power would go to Iran."

"You're right," Deniz nodded her head. "And this all-powerful man was Recep's mentor. Rafsanjani was the link between Romania—with your enlightened leader Ceausescu—and gold."

Deniz removed a faded photo from the drawer. She passed it to Marina. "Ceausescu and Rafsnjani in the 1980s."

"Don't you see?" exclaimed Marina. "Make the connection of what has happened—gold! Ceausescu, gold, Rafsanjani, gold. Recep, gold. The pieces of the puzzle are coming together," she insisted.

Deniz didn't answer. Her body became rigid. She moved slightly away and her demeanor changed, as if she realized she'd been talking too much.

"Thank you for attending my concert," she said politely but distantly. "I hope you enjoy your stay in Istanbul. Tahquitz is a most charming host. He knows everyone who's important in Istanbul." She kissed him good-bye, cheek-to-cheek, asked when they could play backgammon, and walked out of her living room.

At that moment, a middle-aged man with gray hair, very well dressed, walked over to them. "Tahquitz," he said. "I'm so happy to see you. I've missed you."

"Cemele—speak of the devil. Let me introduce you to my friends, Marina and Cristina. This is Cemele Berogan, Istanbul's finest architect."

"You mean the one who's still working despite government crackdowns," he commented and shook everyone's hand. Then turning to Tahquitz, he said, "We have to arrange to play backgammon. I've been practicing."

Tahquitz laughed. "Sounds like a challenge."

"My place? I need you also to help me with my computer. I don't want to give it to anyone in my office to fix. I'm afraid they might copy something confidential."

"I understand. It's safer for me to do it."

"Thanks," Cemele said, and bowed to Marina and Cristina. "Pleased to meet you, ladies. Enjoy Istanbul. Stay out of trouble." He kissed their hands Turkish-style.

"Charming man," Cristina said.

"Yes, and knows the city like no one else. Even the underground of Istanbul."

"Do you mean the caves or the criminals?

"Both."

## 13

*Istanbul, Turkey*
*July 7, 2017*

MARINA, Cristina, and Tahquitz were at the front door of Deniz's house collecting their cellphones from security when Deniz tapped Tahquitz on the shoulder. "I noticed your friends are interested in Recep," she said. "Follow me."

Deniz led them through a dark corridor adjacent to her living room and down a flight of stairs to the basement. When she opened the door, the lights were triggered automatically by sensors. She pressed a button on the wall of the landing and a bookcase slid to the side to reveal another room. Cristina eyed Marina and whispered, "Looks like we're entering something important."

"I don't know if I should be showing you this, but since you're so interested… And I can't talk about with our mutual friends. Somehow it's easier to talk to strangers. This is Recep's secret work area," Deniz said, putting on the light and leading them to the far end of the room. There there were only two pieces of furniture—a chair and large mahogany English desk. Deniz opened the top desk drawer and pressed a button inside a panel, which then exposed several other drawers. She took from the bottom one a jeweled treasure chest the size of a large book.

"Recep thought this secret room was safer than a bank vault." She opened the jeweled box and showed them its contents—two newspaper articles written in English, an envelope, a few photos, some papers, and a tape cassette.

"He guided me through this security system just before we left for Miami. He told me to show these things to the American government if he should get killed."

"Killed?" Cristina said in a whisper. "By whom?"

"Probably a hitman from the Turkish government," Deniz replied sadly. "Just before we left, he had several attempts on his life." She looked down, seemingly reluctant to say more.

"Earlier," commented Marina, "you mentioned that Recep had a pilot's license and flew his own helicopter."

"Yes."

"Well, you said something about a legal loophole to the case, using firefighting helicopters."

"That's right. Sometimes Recep flew the helicopters with his friends from our own backyard." She pointed to the direction of the heliport.

"Why he did he use those helicopters?" Tahquitz asked.

"Recep was following directions from his superiors, and used that legal loophole that allowed shipping food, medicine, and firefighting equipment for humanitarian purposes to Iran, despite their sanctions. He used that loophole to camouflage the gold. And to make sure he had a valid alibi, he specifically used firefighting helicopters to fight so-called fires that he recorded legally."

She took from the treasure chest several photos of the helicopters and showed them the first one.

"Recep had me take the photos because he was so proud. This

one is a Siller Brothers S-64E, a firefighting helicopter equipped with a red Bambi bucket attached to a long cable. The bucket is theoretically used to carry water to extinguish fires, but it can also carry forty tons of heavy cargo."

Tahquitz studied the photo and commented, "I heard that al-Hasadim of Syria had recently used this type of helicopter to transport buckets filled with $100 bills from Damascus to Moscow's Vnukovo Airport. Another reason for Hasadim's friendship with the Russians."

Deniz gave them another photo.

"This is a Kamov KA-32 model used by Iran's Revolutionary Guards' Aviation Corps. It's a Russian design, built to deliver heavy equipment. Its advantage is that it can take off from and land on unpaved ground, like in the mountains. It's also equipped with special guiding lights that cannot be detected from the exterior."

"I've seen helicopters like that in New Mexico when there's a wildfire. It's the same type that the Russians used in the 1980's in Afghanistan to carry Kalashnikov machine guns to their soldiers," said Tahquitz.

"Can I have the photos back? They may be important proof for Recep to make a deal with the Americans," Deniz said.

"Of course. I understand." Tahquitz gave her the photos, which she in turn put back in the treasure chest.

Marina saw a few yellowed papers in the box. "Is there anything else important there that you'd like to show us?"

Deniz hesitated.

"You can trust us," Tahquitz said softly.

"Yes, I'm hoping that… well, that maybe you'll be able to help Recep somehow. I don't tell just anyone these things, you know. But since you live in the US…" She hesitated again, then took out several sheets of paper with graphic markings and a map.

"Recep saved these in case he'd need them. They're air control records that document twenty helicopter flights he flew during the winters of 2011 and 2012. They also record the number of miles he flew for each flight. That's international protocol and must be officially recorded. Recep drew a line from the site of departure in Turkey at Van to the other side of the border in Iran, at the point of arrival, at Tabriz."

She showed them the map.

"If I remember correctly," Tahquitz said, "Recep was born in Tabriz, and his parents still live there. He must know it well."

"That's right," Deniz said. "Flying in the passenger seat next to him as helpers on different occasions were his friends: Belcan, Ozogant's son; Oz Aladek, Ozogant's son-in-law, and the Iranian, Balal Zanssany. They signed in as co-pilots and acted as helpers. All were registered on the records." She passed around the documents of their co-signatures.

"Things went smoothly until 2013, when Recep and his friends were caught on December 17, the night of a thick fog, and were arrested in Istanbul by a police officer and customs official, who —unfortunately—didn't know about their personal ties to Ozogant.

"Some reports claim that the trade transactions amounted to $10 billion worth of gold to Iran from Turkey," Deniz stated. "Other reports came up with an amount of $20 billion or $30 billion. But the key question that hasn't been answered yet is, where did Turkey get gold to start the operation?"

"Right," Tahquitz said. "You cannot wire gold from one bank to another, nor can you use gold certificates. You have to back up gold with hard, tangible gold. Like bars of gold."

"Yes!" Marina said, waving the photos of the firefighting helicopters. "That's the answer to the puzzle. The missing link to the scheme! I believe it was Rafsanjani's gold; but before that, it was Ceausescu's gold bars that started it all."

"A valid theory," Cristina agreed.

"But still a theory," Marina said, disheartened. "There's no proof." She shrugged her shoulders and sighed, frustrated.

"But it makes sense," Deniz insisted. "Bars of gold that Recep transported from Iran to Turkey, which allowed Turkey to then buy Iran's oil with this gold."

"Why?" asked Tahquitz. "It's a cumbersome route. And highly risky."

"It was no doubt worth the risk for Rafsanjani," Deniz said. "He had to get rid of the gold in order to be safe from the Revolutionary Guards. Remember, they're radical and very anti-American. They control most of the businesses in Iran. Rafsanjani was their opponent. He advocated free markets with the West and criticized Iran's restriction of media in Iran because he was heavily invested in tech start-ups. Rafsanjani was coming to the end of his life and wanted peace. He didn't need the money anymore, and wanted to be free of it.

"At the same time," Deniz continued, "he helped Ozogant get elected by making him look good, showing that Ozogant could get gas and oil for a good price and that he could manage the country financially. That's why Ozogant took the gold and arranged the details. Ozogant needed to appear worthy to become president. Recep was his tool."

"I understand your theory," Marina said. "It sounds logical. Most likely, Ozogant had a master plan, since he was Mayor of Istanbul in the mid-90s."

Deniz nodded. "You have to remember that in 2011, when the operation began," she said, "Rafsanjani was losing his former power. The Iranian president at that time, Khorasami, wasn't aware of Rafsanjani's gold dealings in 1989 with Ceausescu. Rafsanjani didn't feel safe disclosing to Khorasami the fact that he had accepted Ceausescu's gold and had hidden it in a private Iranian bank. Rafsanjani never trusted Khorasami. On the other hand, Rafsanjani trusted Rustany, Khorasami's competitor.

Rustany was Rafsanjani's student from the very beginning when they worked together to get rid of the Shah in 1979."

Deniz stopped talking and smiled excitedly. "Look at this photo. Rafsanjani had another student—Recep's best friend!" She took the photo from her treasure chest and passed it around.

"Look at the body language of the two men—how respectful Zanssany is and how Rafsanjani is pleased with such respect."

Deniz stopped talking and looked down. "All these photos, charts, and maps may help Recep if I can get them to someone important in the States—maybe a lawyer or politician."

## 14

*Istanbul, Turkey*
*July 7, 2017*

DENIZ WENT BACK to her desk and took out some more papers and photos from a folder.

"I don't mean to bore you or burden you with family problems." She looked at Tahquitz for reassurance.

"Please, Deniz. We've been friends as well as neighbors for some time now. As as you can see, my friends have already been following this case for quite some time. Boring? It's the most fascinating story I can imagine, and you have a unique perspective. Please go on."

Deniz unfolded two newspaper articles written in Italian and French, with accompanying translations in English. "The first article is about Belcan Ozogant's trip to Bologna. He has an active office in Bologna. Belcan wanted Recep to travel with him, but thankfully, Recep had to stay with me in Istanbul because our daughter had the measles. The article names the president's son in a money laundering investigation in Italy.

"There's also a link about the article in the *Independent* of London."

Deniz paused, gave Tahquitz the Italian newspaper, and said in Italian, "*Chi cerca, trova*—Who searches, finds. This article is about Belcan's arrest in Bologna. He gave an interview to CNN admitting that he left Italy because of allegations. A link to the *Nordic Monitor* explains the case."

She read aloud:

Belcan Ozogant was arrested in Bologna when he brought into Italy large amounts of money in several suitcases. He said he was in Italy to complete a Ph.D. from the University of Bologna's campus of Johns Hopkins University.

Deniz stopped reading for a moment and then continued.

The son of the Turkish President Ozogant is under investigation in Italy for money laundering, in connection, it has been claimed, with the 2013 corruption scandal that rocked the Turkish political establishment.

"The French article is based on a French government investigation that identifies Belcan as a middleman for the Kurds."

"I thought the Turkish government was against the Kurds," Cristina said.

"Yes, theoretically, but Belcan had transported oil from northern Iraq, from the city of Erbil, in 2011, when the Kurdish administration was constructing new pipelines to increase their oil production. This transportation of oil was a secret deal between the Kurds of Erbil and Turkey, and caused a diplomatic rift with Baghdad."

"Why?" Cristina asked.

"The Kurds in northern Iraq are autonomous from other Kurds

and from the Iraqi government. They did what they wanted. But the official government in Baghdad was losing money on these oil deals, while the northern Kurds were making a fortune with Turkey.

"In addition, the government in Baghdad claimed that Turkey was breaching Iraq's constitution, that had been made by the Americans and Iraqi diplomat Adnan Pachachi in 2005. That new constitution specified that all Iraqis, including the northern Kurds, should not sell oil to third parties, like Turkey, without permission from the Iraqi government. The Turkish government blatantly went against this."

"Who was in charge of transporting the oil from Iraq to Turkey?" Tahquitz asked. "That must have been a secret."

"Belcan's transport company managed the operations through his Marinegrande Transportation Corporation to European ports. Both the Kurds from Erbil and Belcan made millions of dollars. The Kurds took their share of the profits and, in turn, bought arms from Ozogant."

"You mean Ozogant, through his son Belcan, was selling arms to the Kurds—whom he hates?" Cristina asked.

"Yes, to Iraqi Kurds from Erbil. It's a specific faction that opposed, at least at that time, other Kurds. These northern Kurds were competitors with other Kurds for oil and power."

"Did Belcan work alone?" Tahquitz asked.

"No. With some friends..." Deniz hesitated to say who. But then added, "Also with his brother-in-law, Oz Aladek.

"They shared a company for transporting oil from Erbil to Turkey via trucks over land and tankers over sea. It was just another business deal for them that they got from Poppa. They've been running the government like a family business."

"Do you know Oz?" Marina asked her.

"Yes, he's been to our house a few times."

"What do you know about him?" Cristina asked, moving closer to Deniz.

"He has a master's degree from New York's Pace University. He married Ozogant's oldest daughter, and afterwards, he became the CEO of Kalleak Holding Group, a Turkish construction and trading company linked to the government. He went on to manage the family network by creating new subsidiaries under Kalleak as the main company. They're all registered in Singapore."

"Do you have proof about Singapore?" Marina asked her.

"Yes, Recep gave me a copy of something." She took out a Danish newspaper from her pile.

"Anything else about this Wizard of Oz?" Cristina wondered.

"Yes. He graduated to become the Minister of Energy and Natural Resources, after bumping off the previous Prime Minister. Talk is that he'll graduate again—to Treasury and Finance Minister. The Turkish Press calls him *damat*–son-in-law. Some critics call him the Clown Prince."

Marina took the article and read the English translation. "These men couldn't have done all of this alone," she commented. "I understand that they were well connected with the Turkish government, but what about the Iranian government?"

"Yes," agreed Tahquitz. "The question is, what was going on from the other side?"

Deniz looked at him, nodded her head, and said, "There was a master puppeteer—the richest man in Iran—Rafsanjani." And she took from her treasure chest for a second time the red copy of *Time* magazine and showed it to them.

"I also have a tape." She took it out to show them her proof.

"What's on the tape?" Cristina asked, eyeing the cassette.

"It's a conversation between Recep and Oz and Belcan, talking about the oil shipments with the Kurds from northern Iraq. Once the voices are identified, they will serve as evidence that Recep was not working alone."

"Where did you get it?" Marina asked.

"My cousin was a policeman. He was dismissed after Recep and his friends were arrested. But his good luck was that Recep dropped his cell phone, and my cousin recognized it as Recep's. It was late at night, dark, and my cousin didn't want another policeman to find Recep's phone. So my cousin took it home for Recep and copied the conversations about shipping oil for the Kurds. He did it as a backup, in case Recep needed it."

"How would that help Recep, though?" Tahquitz asked.

"The voices prove that Recep was pressured by Belcan to work with him. Belcan couldn't risk getting traced and accused of transporting oil for the Kurds and also for a rebel group, or helping Iran bypass sanctions. So Belcan used his friend, Recep, as his front man and pawn. Belcan trusted Recep and tempted him with millions of dollars."

"Recep is still guilty," Marina stated.

"Yes, but if the U.S. government wants information or favors from Turkey, these proofs that I have, can help Recep make a deal with the Americans. Remember, Turkey is near Tabriz, at the Iranian border. The Americans can slip into Iran from Turkey. That may be important one day. Recep can trade what he knows for a new identity and new life in the States, or somewhere else. Then we could have a quiet life together."

"Did Recep do anything else with Belcan for the Turkish government other than the oil shipping?" Tahquitz asked.

"Yes, the gas-for-gold scheme. Belcan worked with Recep to implement the humanitarian loophole with the firefighting helicopters."

Then she hesitated and moved slightly away. But a few seconds later, she changed her mind, and told them, "There's more to the story, but I can't tell it now because I have to talk to the TV camera crew and discuss when my concert will air. I'm so sorry."

"Wait," Tahquitz said, taking her arm. "Don't leave us in the middle of this story. You're acting like Scheherazade. This scheme, gas-for-gold, was it Recep's idea or Ozogant's or Ozogant's son's?"

"Recep had another partner–an Iranian. It was his idea. But that's a long story…" I really can't talk now. She stopped, and then went on to another topic. "I can give you five more minutes."

"Thank you. I don't want to interrupt your work, but…" Tahquitz said.

"One of Recep's roles in all this was to use his contacts with air control officials and customs officials. He made it worth their while not to talk. Recep lived in four countries before I met him: Azerbaijan, Iran, the UAE, and Turkey. He speaks all four languages. EIt was easy for him to offer kickbacks in their language."

"What do you want to do with these newspaper articles and tape?" Marina asked.

"I thought maybe, you, Marina, could make a contact for me in New York. Find me an influential lawyer who could present this information to the American government and help Recep get protection and make a deal."

"Help him make a deal?" Cristina asked, surprised. "How?"

"An important lawyer could tell the truth that Recep was forced by the Ozogant family, as well as by the Iranian and Turkish governments, to handle the shipping of oil for the Kurds and rebels, and to take blame for the gas-for-gold scheme."

"What happens if the American government or the FBI have emails or wiretaps, also of Recep's voice, talking to accomplices about his deals? And the information is different from yours? And maybe the FBI knew what was going on all along," Marina said. "The wiretaps could show that Recep willingly got involved. That he wasn't forced."

"I know he was forced!" Deniz protested.

She took a sheet of paper out of its envelope. "This letter is also proof that he was coerced. And now, I have to go."

The letter was written in Turkish, but Tahquitz took it and tried a rough translation:

```
Dear Recep,

The bird that flies too high is easily
shot down.
Through my bird-hunter contacts, I've
heard that you've forgotten the meaning of
loyalty.

You should not forget what my father and I
have done for you. A bird carrier of
secrets can't fly too far and must be
caught in hand.
```

Tahquitz put the letter back in its envelope. Deniz disappeared, leaving the group to wonder what it all meant.

---

Deniz finally returned, looking surprised that they were still there.

"Did you get the television scheduled sorted out?" Tahquitz asked.

"Yes, they're working on it. Looks like it will air tomorrow." Deniz looked distracted.

"Can you please explain more about the letter?" Cristina asked. "It seems rather mysterious."

"Okay. When Recep received this letter, hand-delivered from Belcan's gardener with a dead bird in the envelope, he got scared. The bird had a small Iranian flag knotted around its neck. When Recep showed it to me, he said, 'They caught my Iranian friend. We have to take a trip to the States.'"

Marina, Cristina, and Tahquitz were silent.

After a long pause, Deniz continued, "If the Americans want information to use against the Iranians for bypassing sanctions, and proof against the Turkish government for being accomplices, then they might cut a deal with Recep. If they offer him safety, he could give them some important information. I know Recep. He would like a quiet life with me and Astara. That's why he went to Miami. He knew they'd free me, and he could try to make a deal."

"Maybe he's already spoken about these schemes to the American government," Marina reasoned. "He's been in a New York prison for more than a year. Plenty of time to talk."

"Yes, but I have all these papers as *proof!*" Deniz insisted. "He can't get this information that he hid in the desk, because he's in jail and he doesn't want to tell them about me—that I have the papers. He's protecting me. But these papers could make a difference for a deal and his release."

Marina shrugged. "I don't know if the Americans would make a deal with him. He *is* guilty."

Deniz looked down at her feet. Cristina moved closer to her. "Forgive me for asking, but a woman's curiosity..." She hesitated.

Deniz gave her an encouraging look to continue.

"Why did you marry Recep in the first place? You must have realized that so much money in such a short time was suspicious."

"Yes, but I was taken by his *joie de vivre*. He loves life so much that it was contagious. He made me happy."

Marina smiled, took Tahquitz's hand, and squeezed it.

Deniz continued talking about Recep. "He'd wake up in the morning, full of energy, and want to make love. Then afterwards, on the pillow, he'd whisper to me, 'I want so much to give you pleasure. Let's take my helicopter to Cappadocia for lunch and have salted fire fish. Or travel to the Mediterranean and have dinner in my yacht. Or race my Ferrari and Aston Martin.' I was impressed he was able to do all these things, and was so sophisticated."

Deniz stopped talking and took Recep's envelope and, closing her eyes, she stroked her cheeks with it.

Marina stared at her. Recep's behavior was so different from what Marina knew or believed in. Were his actions frivolous? High risk? And did she have the right to judge him?

Cristina, on the other hand, was still curious, and asked Deniz, "How did you meet Recep? I'm fascinated by such an unusual character, even if I know he has a dark side. A little like an anti-hero."

"Our story is a love story," Deniz said, as tears fell down her cheeks. She took a photo from a desk drawer and showed it to them. "This was taken at the wedding of Mohammad, his brother, when we first met. Some mutual friends introduced us. I remember how shy Recep was. He couldn't speak. He just stared at me. He wanted to ask me to dance but he was too inhibited. The next day, his friend came to my house with a package from Recep. He had written two love songs for me as a gift." She smiled, remembering. "They became my biggest hits. How could I not fall for him? It's exciting to know such a brilliant man loves you!"

"I understand," Marina agreed, smiling at Tahquitz.

Then Tahquitz asked, "So why did you file for divorce?"

"In order to be an important singer in Turkey, I needed government support. An official called me to his office when I returned from Miami and told me if I want to give another concert, I'd have to divorce Recep. They wanted to put all the blame on him for the gas-for-gold scheme and keep the American government and journalists away from Belcan and his father."

"Don't tell me you worked for the Turkish government?" Marina asked, horrified.

"Not at all. I didn't tell them anything they didn't already know. I just made them believe I was on their side."

Deniz turned to Cristina. "What should I do?"

"Can you photocopy all the documented papers, letters, newspaper articles, and translations for me? I'll show them to someone who can advise me what to do." Cristina hesitated and then said, "I trust him–my husband."

"I have a Xerox machine upstairs."

"Good, and I'll make the phone call."

Cristina held on tightly to the *Time* magazine in her hand. But she couldn't forget what Deniz had said about Recep's Iranian friend. What had Recep been doing with his Iranian friend to get so scared that he went to Miami to get arrested?

# 15

*Istanbul, Troy, Pergamum, and Ephesus, Turkey*
*July 8, 2017*

THE NEXT DAY AT BREAKFAST, Marina, Cristina, and Tahquitz chatted incessantly about Deniz, Recep, and their friends. Cristina was adamant that she'd try to help—or at least ask Eugen for his opinion. She said she had tried to call him several times in Paris, but he didn't answer his cellphone or his private Blackberry. Frustrated, she left several messages.

To change the mood, Tahquitz suggested the possibility of taking a trip while they waited for Eugen to return Cristina's call.

"I'd love to show you both Pamukkale—a very special place." Turning to Cristina, he told her, "We can pass by a factory showroom that you'd love. The owner is my sister's friend. They make the pillows you admired in the living room and at Deniz's house."

Cristina remembered how much she liked the silk fabric with golden thread and hand-embroidered tulips in various colors. The reds blended into oranges that turned into yellows and then greens appeared, like a kaleidoscope of purple-bluish flowers.

She had first seen the style in Santa Fe at the Inn. "Maybe they have a variety of fabrics. I could design a Turkish fashion show." Her imagination was already planning.

"I'll call for an appointment," he told her. "And Marina, Pamukkale has something for you—a group of hot springs and mineral waters. Your fountain of youth. I'd love to see you feel the mineral waters on your beautiful face."

She laughed and gave him an endearing smile.

"The waters are a national treasure in Turkey," he explained, "but their wonder is a secret from the rest of the world."

"Just what you're searching for," Cristina commented, sensing Marina's curiosity.

"I know someone in the industry," Tahquitz told them, "who lives and works there. His business is mineral waters, but what he does is unique: he mixes scents and flavors into the liquid. He's very successful, but he keeps his market domestic. He says it's easier that way to keep an eye on his secrets. But we're good friends."

Marina understood that being friends in Turkey meant trust. She stared at Tahquitz when he said his last few words. He was wearing a pale blue shirt that was tight-fitting around the waist, and he looked strong and muscular. "Are you implying that you'll entice him to work with us?" She smiled.

He gave her his mischievous grin that she liked so much. "It's for you to decide if you like what he says."

She didn't answer, but she felt she was being offered an opportunity to see more of Tahquitz in Turkey, a side of him that she liked. It was easier for her to get closer to him in Istanbul, a city where he seemed more comfortable than in New York.

*Who knows—fate—new energy with an exciting man who is different and fun. It's been too many years*, she tried to reason with herself, *since Stefan.* If she hadn't her friends and work, she would have never been able to go on without Stefan. And now, Tahquitz has entered her life by a chance encounter. Or was it destiny? She sensed there was something telling her to grab the opportunity and not be afraid. There was something about Tahquitz that reminded her of Stefan. The way he smiled at her—flirting and teasing, as if he were playing, yet challenging her. And his goodness. She wondered if it was not too late in her life for a second chance.

"Is Pamukkale far?" Cristina asked. Her timing of when to interject some words was appreciated by Marina, who was trying to understand her inner feelings.

"Yes and no," Tahquitz answered, moving closer to Marina, and silently taking her hand. *Maybe he's sensing my pensive mood*, she thought, *and wants to tell me to trust him.*

"A couple days' ride by car," he said, "and a lovely trip to the Aegean. We can leave in the morning. My car is ready."

"I'd love that," Marina answered and she turned to Cristina."What do you say?"

"For sure!"

"I thought we could also stop along the way and visit some historical sights—Troy, then Pergamum, spending the night near there, then on the next day to Ephesus and Pamukkale around sunset. The next day we can visit the factory. It's near my friend's house."

"How exciting!" Marina hugged him. He was like Aladdin, using his magic carpet to fly them away.

"We'll be able to visit towns that mix Turkish and Greek history from two thousand years ago," he explained. "There were no borders then. Aristotle lived a while in what's now Turkey, and so did the Virgin Mary, who lived in Ephesus."

"I'll bring my sketch book," Cristina responded. "I'm sure I'll be inspired. And I'm thinking—there's an old Roman amphitheater in Paris near rue Monge in the Latin Quarter that would make a great backdrop and stage for a fashion show."

Her friends laughed.

"I'll bring my camera," Marina said, hoping she'd find some herbs that didn't grow anywhere else.

"And I'll bring my guide books," Tahquitz added, smiling.

---

Early the next morning, packed, equipped, and eager, they set out for their road trip. Stopping first at Troy, they marveled that there was actually a horse made of wood guarding the city's main entrance. Tahquitz took pictures of Marina and Cristina standing next to the ladder as Marina teased, "Beware of women bearing gifts."

He replied by taking a dozen photos.

They continued south toward Izmir for Pergamum. Tahquitz had suggested they park the car and enter Pergamum's site through a lesser known gate that he had used when a teenager. This would take them through a path lined with ancient marble stones and Doric columns that opened up to an *agora,* a market place, which was flanked with stone remnants of ancient shops. As they walked, they passed under a high altar about ten feet tall that extended the length equal to several streets. The overhead altar was constructed from flat stones that had small, perforated holes. Tahquitz explained they were walking through a type of tunnel—the entrance to *Asklepieion*—the foremost medical center of the ancient world. The holes were for eyes, where doctors and scholars secretly observed the new patients as they entered the gates.

"This was the very start of psychiatry," Tahquitz told them. "Doctors studied the behavior of a patient without being noticed and then discussed the case amongst themselves. The ancients were behaviorists, believing body language could explain a patient's inner world."

As the three friends walked past the remains of the medical clinic, they found the famous library of Pergamum. "Supposedly, two centuries before Christ," he explained, "this library contained 200,000 manuscripts that were written on very thin parchment and were rolled up and stored in reading rooms. Legend states that Mark Anthony gave Cleopatra all of the 200,000 scrolls from Pergamum for the Library at Alexandria in Egypt as a wedding present."

"Wow!" Cristina said as Marina took photos. "Imagine, this was the greatest source of knowledge at that time, and it was accidentally burned in war."

"Yes, the library was the beginning of civilized culture. But let me show you something that's not in any guide book."

He led them down a path created by flat, white stones into a hidden chamber. "Be careful; look down as you walk. Take note of the indentations in the stones. It was a system for water to flow in and out of this room that was used for Baths." He pointed to a large square chamber ahead of them made of flat, thin rocks. "Rain and water over centuries have made these special rocks smooth so they retain humidity for the baths."

"You mean baths to clean yourself, like the famous Turkish baths?"

"Yes, for aristocrats. The baths comprised the first room, which led to the library that led to a series of small chambers." He pointed to lines of stones in rectangular shapes. "Each chamber was a room in a brothel."

"You mean the baths connected to the library and then to a whorehouse?" Cristina asked, surprised.

He laughed. "This secret complex dates back to 2,000 years ago. An aristocrat would tell his wife that he was going to read in the library. He'd enter through the tunnel we just passed to the reading room, and then he'd sneak away to the baths, clean himself, and enter the brothel. Afterwards, he'd return to the baths, wash himself again, and return to his books."

"And then to his wife," Marina joked.

Cristina laughed. "As Tahquitz said, the beginning of civilization."

They lingered a while amidst the ancient stones and spoke of the lost world that was no longer. "Were people happier then?" Marina asked.

Tahquitz whispered to her, "No one could be happier than I am now."

Cristina walked away, diplomatically, to sketch the flow of ancient rooms.

Tahquitz broke the silence. "The tour is not over. Tomorrow is Ephesus and the temple of the Virgin Mary, *Meryemana,* where it's said that Jesus's mother lived her last days."

They found a simple but comfortable inn nearby and spent the night.

They got an early start the next morning. After arriving, they walked to the harbor to find a simple, one-room stone house. They toured the shrine in respectful silence, and then stepped out into the warm morning sunshine.

Cristina pointed to a wall outside covered with strips of material that had been tied to it. "What is that?" she asked.

"That's the wishing wall," explained a guide who came up behind them, leading a small tour group. His English was excellent, and he seemed enthusiastic to explain the site to anyone interested. "People write wishes or prayers on slips of paper or cloth, tie them to the wall, in the hopes they'll come true. Would you like to try?"

Both women enthusiastically agreed, and Tahquitz bought them strips of cloth from a souvenir stand.

"What did you wish for?" he asked Marina, after she'd tied her contribution. But she just smiled.

"We should hurry on to EEphesus now," Tahquitz said. "It's a large site, and it takes some time to explore."

"Wasn't Ephesus originally part of Greece?" Marina asked, as they drove.

"Yes, it was founded in the 10$^{th}$ century B.C.E. by the ancient Greeks. And in ten centuries, it belonged to several Empires—Roman, Byzantine, Persian, and early Christian. The Apostles, Paul and John, lived there. Jesus asked John to take care of his mother after his death, in Ephesus."

"I remember from my art studies of classical archaeology," interjected Cristina, "that in the 14$^{th}$ century, Ephesus became part of the Ottoman Empire."

"What a history," Marina said.

At the site, they paid their entrance fares and readied their cameras. Every angle seemed to present a photo opportunity more striking than the last.

"We studied ancient Greek civilization in school," Cristina remarked. "It's amazing to be actually stepping now on those very same places I first saw in my history book."

They continued exploring until the end of the day, when Tahquitz suggested they take a detour to an ancient acropolis where Alexander the Great had once stayed. Tahquitz looked at his watch and said they could see the sunset there before continuing on to Pamukkale to his friend's home for dinner. Tahquitz had several small flashlights in his backpack and handed them to Marina and Cristina, who playfully pretended they were fire torches.

They proceeded up a maze of narrow dirt paths that were rarely traveled because of their steepness and the large boulders that blocked the way. Determined to continue on, they came to an opening where there had once been an agora and was now marked by ancient stones. From there, a steep, slippery path took them to another opening in the hillside where the remains of a semi-circular Greek theater was protected by six Doric columns. The three friends paused to look down to a stone aqueduct spanning the length of a verdant hill.

They sat down on the grass, tired from the upward hike, and without speaking, admired the view of history surrounding them. The sun began to set, and Marina held out her hands as if she wanted to touch the sky. Red, orange, and yellow colors streaked the ancient rocks in a mysterious cloak. Within seconds, sparks of white light sparkled the sky silver. Far below was the blue sea of the Aegean, while above, clouds colored the fields in a crimson mist. Time stood still as the beauty encircling her blended into golden hues. She felt an inner peace within her.

As night came quickly, the three friends climbed downwards with their flashlights, barely speaking for fear they'd lose the feeling of beauty that had overcome them.

Suddenly, out of the dark hills, an elderly man emerged, walking slowly. He stopped and greeted them in Turkish and then said, "I am blind."

Tahquitz translated his words to Marina and Cristina.

"I cannot see what others see, but I can see what others cannot see. And as I feel your presence, three good friends, I feel you will find a secret, a truth, that you did not know before. But before you find it, you might suffer."

Tahquitz remained silent, hesitating if he should translate the words to his companions. Then he saw Marina's inquisitive look and knew he didn't want to lie to her. After he interpreted the prophecy, everyone was quiet.

The blind man moved to leave, and Tahquitz said, "I'm very moved by your words."

"You will find a way. Your goodness will guide you."

Tahquitz did not translate those words. Instead he took the man's arm. "Can I help you walk this narrow path?"

"How kind of you. No need. This is my private world. I know my way."

"Is there anything we can do for you?" Tahquitz asked.

"I was going to ask what I can do for you. Would you like me to read your palms?"

"Read?" Tahquitz asked, surprised.

"Not actually *read,* but I can feel the lines. I am sensitive to that, and I have studied the creases of life. The left palm tells your past, what you were before you started your present life. You might say, your potential. The right palm tells of achievement in the present and what you may become in the future."

Tahquitz turned to Marina and Cristina and translated. "Would you like that?"

They both shook their heads no.

The old man did not understand their English, but he sensed their reticence and answered, "You are right. I have already told you enough about your future. Let me pray your sufferings will be short." He pronounced a blessing in a language Tahquitz did not know and in Turkish, wished them good luck. Continuing on his way, the blind man climbed over boulders with a calm that harmonized with the ancient setting around him.

## 16

*Pamukkale, Turkey*
*July 9, 2017*

THE NEXT MORNING, the three friends awoke in Pamukkale where they had stayed the night at the home of Tahquitz's friend Erol Hasslan.

Pamukkale was a wonder to wake up to. As they ate their breakfast outdoors in Erol's terraced garden, they admired the surrounding pools of mineral waters made up of different depths and colors. Cristina commented that it seemed they were in the middle of a natural wonder where the stones surrounding the pools looked like sliced gemstones and the multicolored springs flowed in a rippling architectural design. She was busy sketching the different colored stones mixing with the crystal water.

Marina asked Erol if after breakfast, she could visit his laboratory and learn about the different scents he made from herbs and flowers.

He beamed with pride. "My pleasure," he replied, but he made no attempt to rush. Instead, he said, he first wanted to talk to them about something he had just learned. He stood up from the table and walked around several pools of gemstoned waters, thinking of how to begin.

"I heard Deniz gave a concert the other night."

"Yes," Tahquitz replied. "It was very creative. A very different style of singing as percussion for her. Highly effective."

"I saw it on TV," Erol replied. "How is she? I haven't seen her in a while. I realize she's preoccupied, but I miss her." He paused and then said in a lower voice, "I knew Recep."

Marina and Cristina moved closer to Erol.

"He's very cunning for a young man," he commented. "Recep was trained well."

"What do you mean?" Marina asked.

"Trained by his best friend, Balal Zanssany, who's about ten years older than he. Does the name mean anything to you?" he asked, turning to Tahquitz, who stood up at that moment to join Erol.

"Yes and no."

Erol explained. "Zanssany got arrested at the end of December of 2013 in Tehran, a couple of weeks after he and Recep were detained at Istanbul's airport. Zanssany never had a trial, but the Iranian government found him guilty of corruption, embezzlement, forgery of documents and bank statements, and money laundering. He's still in prison. Maybe Deniz spoke of him?"

"Not by name," Tahquitz replied. He seemed surprised that Erol knew so much about the case.

"Was Zanssany a close friend of Recep's?" Marina asked, interested in anyone or anything related to Sharatt.

"Yes, they were always together. Zanssany was the leader of the group, followed by Belcan Ozogant, Hamza Caglyan, Balal Gul, and Oz Boreck, all sons of ministers. But since 2013, no more."

Erol picked up two stones and brushed them together. "All these young men, once a group of best friends, now rubbing against each other, pulled apart by the gas-for-gold scandal. Each one against the other to save his own skin."

Erol paused. No one said a word, but they encouraged him with their interest to continue.

"In 2013, when Zanssany was arrested, he was thirty-nine years old. He was worth over thirteen billion dollars and was the managing director of the Sorayanne Group, one of Iran's largest business conglomerates, which includes something like sixty-five companies doing business in several countries. He started out very modestly, first selling sheepskins as a boy, then went on to college and earned a business degree in crisis management."

"Sounds like that diploma came in handy for him," Marina commented.

"Yes, he went on to solve one crisis after another. He used his cunning and personality to climb to the top. He was very handsome, with fine reddish hair, fair skin, and piercing blue eyes. He's also brilliant, speaking many languages, and traveling the world. He had a magnetic personality with many sides to his character. His Facebook page shows a gentle side, playing the violin. And yet, there was something very arrogant about him. When he was interrogated by Iran's Ministry of Oil about his debts, he denied any wrongdoing, claiming, 'I prospered because of God's help.'

"Zanssany thought he was smarter than everyone else and could do whatever he wanted. He was accused and imprisoned for withholding nearly three billion dollars in commissions from what he had collected on behalf of the Iranian government and Ministry of Oil in the gas-for-gold scandal with Turkey."

"How was he part of that?" Marina asked.

"He was the brains. Even the Iranian government, including Khorasami who was president at the time, gave him *carte blanche* to proceed as he wanted, as long as he'd bypass international sanctions and collect the money for the government.

"He began in 2010 by trading and selling oil for the Ministry as their broker. He insisted that he never took more than his commission of .007%. Yet Zanssany was accused by the European Union of being the key facilitator for the illegal Iranian oil deals and laundering the oil-related money. He denied the accusations and called it a mistake.

"But it wasn't a mistake. His work was very intentional and precise. He transferred millions of oil barrels from tanker to tanker in a remote location, far from anyone's eyes. He used a small, little-known harbor on the tiny Malaysian island of Labuan. In total, he sold 24 million barrels of oil to buyers in Singapore, Malaysia, and India. Recep told me that the bank Zanssany used, the Malay Premier Bank, is on the U.S. sanctions list.

"It was Sharatt who transferred billions to his companies abroad for his friend. Sharatt moved the money between Hachebanque, the government's official bank, and Hactive Bank, the largest private investment firm in Turkey. Then he arranged for the banks to convert the cash to gold and transfer it to a privately owned bank in Tehran." He paused. "*Which* private bank is a big question. I never figured that one out."

Erol's listeners didn't comment. They couldn't speak. They could hardly breathe.

"Zanssany is the interesting link, the silent one behind the scenes," Erol said. "The young Turks involved in the gas-for-gold scheme were released from prison after two months when President Ozogant finally stepped in. But Zanssany was never released from Evin Prison in Tehran. After three years in jail, on March 6, 2016, he was formally convicted and sentenced to death. The Iranian government put all the blame on him to avoid the E.U., U.S. and U.N. decision that Iran was guilty of circumventing the embargo.

"The Iranian government, to prove their innocence, presented in court a indictment against Zanssany that was over two-hundred pages long and based on thirty to forty meetings with Zanssany, as well as several trips by Iranian officials to Malaysia, Dubai, and Tajikistan to locate the missing money. The government was searching for proof against him and also looking for the money. But they couldn't find anything. He's still in prison. The money is still missing; the blame is still on him."

"*He became the fall guy,*" whispered Cristina.

"Yes," echoed Erol. "You know what his conviction was? Corruption against the earth. Punishment by hanging."

"Is that a joke?" Cristina asked.

"No. You can look it up."

Everyone was silent.

"Deniz told me she's afraid that Recep may know where the money is," Erol said, breaking the silence. "He told her that when everything is all over, he dreams of taking her to Dubai."

"You seem to know a lot about this case," Marina said.

Erol nodded his head, looked down, and didn't comment further. But after several seconds he started again.

"Because of Zanssany, Iran's oil industry changed their entire operation to avoid being traced and accused of bypassing international sanctions. They didn't want to repeat their past mistakes. And they didn't want to lose their future oil revenue."

"What do you mean?" Marina asked him.

"I have a cousin who is Iranian. He used to work in Iran's oil industry as a broker until he got sick." Erol looked away for a moment and then continued. "He explained to me how their oil industry is run, like a spy agency."

The three listeners were quiet. They waited, staring at Erol, imploring him silently to say more.

"Because of Zanssany, the Ministry of Petroleum got rid of dozens of brokers. Couldn't trust them. Even had a hand-full jailed; claimed they were spies. That they leaked information about sales and clients.

"To redress the problem, the government consolidated all transactions into the hands of four retired generals from the Revolutionary Guards. The brokers who remained working could not sell directly anymore to a client-country. They could only recommend if the buyer was trustworthy. If he was proven to be so, the Iranian broker would then send a proposal to one of the four officials. One was in charge of China, another of Syria, another of India, and another of Europe. The broker brought the client to a secret location, and there the chief official discussed price, payment, and shipping. An overseas bank account was opened at that moment and then closed within an hour once the transaction was completed. The broker, during this time, was guarded in a room where he was served kebabs and Chinese tea. His cell phone was confiscated during the transaction. Once the deal was finished, he got back his phone, and the broker and client left separately."

"Sounds like a spy thriller," Cristina said.

"There's more," Erol commented. "All cell phones were copied, and documents from sales had to be put into hard copy, scanned, and then discarded."

"Sounds like the oil information was guarded as war information."

"Exactly. Iran against America."

"*Realpolitik*," Tahquitz commented. "Let's connect the dots and go from oil to gas to gold. From Zanssany to Sharatt. How do you see all this?" he asked Erol.

"It's a clear picture," Erol said, snapping his fingers as if the answer was obvious. "I can crystallize the picture for you, if you want more."

"Actually," Marina said, "no need. We've actually been following this case closely, and know many of the details."

"Yes," Tahquitz said. "Basically, Iran has gas and oil. Turkey needs gas and oil. Iran is blocked from selling because of sanctions due to their nuclear program. Turkey can't pay Iran because of sanctions, and so gold comes into the picture."

"But the question is," Erol adds, "where did they get so much gold? And where did the gold come from to start the operation? That's the missing clue to the puzzle."

"Wait," Marina said, pacing the garden floor. "You have to think out of the box. Include some dates as clues to this puzzle. In March of 2016, Zanssany was formally sentenced to death despite the fact that he was in Evin prison for more than three years."

"Yes," Erol agreed.

Marina continued. "Recep and Deniz entered Miami thirteen days after Zanssany was sentenced to be hanged. That can't be a coincidence."

"You're right," Cristina said. "Sharatt got scared. He was afraid he'd become the fall guy for President Ozogant. The Turkish government would get the idea from the Iranians."

"Yes. Don't forget what Deniz told us—that there were several attempts on Recep's life from the Turkish government."

"From the Iranian government also, I'm afraid," Erol said. "They claim that Zanssany's debt of almost three billion dollars fell into Sharatt's hands. If Sharatt returns the money, his friend can go free."

"No wonder Recep got frightened at hearing Zanssany's death sentence," Marina said.

"So Sharatt's master scheme was not gas-for gold," Tahquitz concluded, "but to get arrested in the States and then make a deal with the American government to get protection. He's not only afraid of the Turkish leader but also of the Iranians. He must have some very valuable information about Iran and Turkey. I wonder what it is? And if he knows from where the gold came from originally."

"And if he really knows where his friend's billions are, as the Iranian government claims he does."

## 17

*New York City and Paris*
*Autumn 2017*

MARINA AND CRISTINA planned to return to Istanbul at the end of autumn. Marina wanted to follow up on Erol's experiments with mineral waters to be used with skin creams. If the waters retained their fragrance and continued to hydrate the skin, she planned to ship samples back to New York and experiment further. Marina was also in discussion with Turkish glass makers about how to create bottles in tulip shapes for the new cosmetic line, after being inspired by the apple tea served in tulip-shaped glasses. Tahquitz was arranging meetings for her near Istanbul.

Cristina wanted to follow up in person about the fabrics she had chosen for her Parisian designs. She was excited about her modern interpretation of Turkish harem pants, full and loose-fitting, made of silk with embroidered flowers and gold thread that enhanced the flowers' texture and shine. It was important for her to check on the stitching quality of the fabrics before they started cutting the designs. She had already booked the fashion show in Paris at Les Arènes de Lutèce, an ancient Roman colosseum that was used ages ago as an amphitheater. June thirtieth was her target date, when Paris would be in the middle of blooming flowers and sunshine.

The two friends spoke on the phone almost every other day to discuss their business plans and to chat about their lives. But what fascinated them the most was to share thoughts about Recep, Deniz, and all the Turkish and Iranian players involved in the gas-for-gold case. Periodically there'd be a report from Finland that they aired simultaneously on their computers and commented on while watching.

Particularly interesting to them was a vlog episode about Rafsanjani that was presently flashing on their computer screens while they were on the phone together.

The transmission started with a photo of Zanssany, very similar to the one that Deniz had shown them from her treasure chest, when he was receiving an award from Rafsanjani.

"Why is Rafsanjani so pleased?" Marina asked Cristina on the phone, while watching her screen.

"It looks like Rafsanjani is pulling the strings of his young marionette who's in awe in front of him," Cristina replied. "Remember, Rafsanjani was the richest man in Iran. Just what Zanssany dreamt of being!"

"And then Khorasami, who's in power, punishes them all," Marina summarized. "Locks up Zanssany, cuts the strings of the master puppeteer, Rafsanjani, and cuts Rustany's powers for the future. Gets rid of his competition."

Suddenly on the computer screen flashed two photos and the narrator's voice.

*Viewers, please look at these pictures that we are posting to illustrate the real power in Iranian politics. The first photo shows Ayatollah Camaney with Ayatollah Rafsanjani and President*

*Rustany. The second photo is of President Rustany with his long-time mentor, Rafsanjani.*

Marina and Cristina sat mesmerized in front of their computer screens as the narrator filled in the background to the images they were viewing.

*We want to show you how power from Iran has extended halfway around the globe to Argentina. We want to give you a complete portrait of Rafsanjani from another angle to illustrate how power politics can turn evil.*

*The first article we're summarizing gives an overview of the topic. It appeared in the New York Times on November 10, 2006, with the title "Argentina Seeks Arrest of Iran's Ex-Leader in 1994 Bombing Inquiry."*

*An Argentine judge ordered international arrest warrants on Thursday for a former Iranian president Ali Akbar Hashemi Rafsanjani and eight others in connection with the 1994 bombing of a Jewish community center in Buenos Aires. This has been declared the most tragic terrorist attack in Argentine history.*

*Argentine prosecutors have formally accused the Iranian government—specifically Ayatollah Camaney and Ayatollah Rafsanjani—of master-minding the attack, which killed eighty-five people and wounded more than two hundred.*

*Iran has denied any involvement in the blast of July 18, 1994, when a truck filled with explosives leveled the Argentine Israeli Mutual Association building, a cultural center and symbol of the country's Jewish population, which is South America's largest.*

*No one has been convicted formally of carrying out the attack despite a lengthy investigation marked by accusations of judicial misconduct and government cover-ups. But Argentine, Israeli, and American officials have long blamed the Lebanese group Hezbollah, which is backed by Iran.*

*The attack was one of two on Argentina's Jewish population during the 1990's. A March 1992 blast at the Israeli Embassy in Buenos Aires killed twenty-nine people, an attack also that remains also unsolved.*

*In court documents, Argentine prosecutors say the attack on the community center of 1994 could have been tied to Argentina's decision to stop providing Iran with nuclear technology and materials, and Argentina suspended their contract of nuclear research with Iran.*

*Several Rafsanjani associates are being sought. Mr. Rafsanjani was Iran's president from 1989 to 1997 and remains a powerful figure in his country."*

*The second article is an article that will appear next week in the New York Times. It will have as its title: "Iranian Terror. Argentinian Cover Up. Justice at Last."*

*The article will discuss a full investigation of these terrorist attacks, centering on Hector Richner, President of Argentina from 2003-2007, and his wife Prissy Fernandez de Richner, President of Argentina from 2007-2015. There has been a mysterious murder of the case's chief prosecutor, Alberto Nisman. Evidence points to Prissy Richner's role in the homicide.*

*Nisman had formally accused the government of Iran of directing*

*the 1994 bombing and the Hezbollah militia of carrying it out.*
*This act of violence was Argentina's most deadly terrorist attack*
*in the 20th century.*

*Nisman, who was Jewish, was personally motivated to find out the*
*truth about the attack. Nisman had researched the case for years*
*to gather evidence to blame Iran for its involvement. One day*
*before he was to present his 300-page report in court on Monday,*
*January 18, 2015, he was found dead in his apartment on Sunday*
*January 17.*

Marina could hardly hold the phone in her hand. "What do you think of that?"

"All true. I remember the case. I read about how the Archbishop of Buenos Aires at the time was outraged at the two bombings and started a public investigation."

"Who was he?" Cristina asked.

"Our present Pope Francis, Jorge Mario Bergoglio, from Buenos Aires. In 2005, when he was Cardinal, he was the first public personality to sign a petition for justice in the case. As part of the bombing's 11th anniversary, he was the leading signatory of the document called, "85 victims, 85 signatures.""

"What was the result of the investigation?" Marina asked.

"It's still ongoing. Cristina Richner has been indicted and is still being investigated for her role in Nisman's homicide."

"It's a web of crime. One criminal leads to another, one story involves another, one country to another. Even in the U.S. Where will it stop? The more we dig, the more evil we find."

"Let's hope we stay out of it."

"I'll say a prayer for that," Marina commented.

"Until then," Cristina said, "I have to go for now. Speak to you soon."

# 18

*Istanbul, Turkey*
*November 27, 2017*

THE FRIENDS ARRIVED in Istanbul the day after Thanksgiving, Marina from New York City and Cristina from Paris. They stayed at Tahquitz's house. His sister and her husband were still in Ankara on business and Tahquitz had taken time off from his clinic on the reservation in Taos to join the women in Istanbul.

On this particular morning, they left Tahquitz after breakfast, for he had some meetings to arrange for Marina. Cristina was eager to take a walk through the city while he did his phoning. Tahquitz suggested that she and Marina visit the Blue Mosque, and from there, they could all meet for lunch at a specific café he knew near Taksim Square.

He called a taxi so they could begin at Florya Sahil Yolu, a section parallel to the Sea of Marmara. But more quickly than they expected, the driver arrived while Marina was still getting ready, hunting for her boots.

"Why do you want to wear boots?" Cristina asked her. "It doesn't look like it'll rain."

"You never know. The weather changes quickly here. And they're my most comfortable shoes. I presume we'll be walking a lot."

"Should we take an umbrella?"

"No, we're wearing hats, and I hate carrying one."

"Let's go. The driver is waiting."

The early morning was still misty before the sun could break free the fog. They passed several mosques that blended as chiaroscuro counterparts to the sea. It appeared as if the land of Europe from where they were walking to the opposite Asian side of Usküdar was a blur of mystery, two continents encircled in a fragile fog.

They strolled, admiring multiple minarets and listened to the chants of muezzins like Sirens calling the devout to prayer. From the rooftops, the chants echoed from one mosque to another like a chorus from Heaven, while below, men were scurrying toward their mosque to pray. Istanbul took on a magical quality in the cloak of mist and music from the morning's beginning.

In contrast, the Sea of Marmara was choppy, and they marveled at how the ferryboats could forge forward despite such high waves and strong currents. Neighboring islands appeared like bumps in the sea, and in the distance there was a faint silhouette of a light-house perched on a faraway land. Boats traveled from one island to the other as they had for hundreds of years. Weather didn't detour them, nor did the tides of history. And yet, they had to take warning that the sky was ominous, and the day could change.

"The ancient Turks and Greeks used to pray at these waterways before they'd set sail to travel," Marina said.

"I can understand why. Look at the clouds up there—the winds change fast here. Nature is stronger than man."

Marina commented that the waterways in Istanbul were part of legends. "Jason and his Argonauts sailed in search of the Golden Fleece from here to go through the Bosphorus."

Cristina smiled. "Gold. It seems we're still searching for that—man's treasure hunt. Even us."

"Something of a hallucinatory mystery in this mist. Homer described how the fog brings all parts of the city together to become one. It looks like the Bosphorus has the key to two worlds and two cultures—Istanbul is the link."

"I once read that Zeus fell in love with Hera in these waters. I wonder if she knew from the beginning that she'd be Queen." They both laughed.

Marina and Cristina strolled parallel to the waterways and chatted about Deniz and Recep and their circle of friends. They were puzzled as to whether Recep had hidden or spent or even ever possessed Zanssany's billions. Would Zanssany pay his debts to the Iranian government to get out of jail? And what about the gold? Where had it come from originally? How could one be sure? The secret, as the gold, was shared by Ceausescu and Rafsanjani—two souls lost, but not forgotten, in the fog.

Marina wondered if there were a flip side to genius—a negative superiority that made a genius feel he could do anything, even commit a crime. Did they get bored so easily that they needed more thrills? She remembered as a student how fascinated she had been with Dostoyevsky's *Crime and Punishment*. She'd obsessed over the concept of motive and guilt, and how far the genius thought he could go without limits or without justice. And now Cristina was questioning whether they should try to help Recep, as Deniz had asked them.

"Help a criminal expose another criminal to save his skin? Is that ethical? Legal? Should we get involved?"

"I do know a criminal lawyer in New York," Marina replied, thinking out loud. "Someone I could consult for advice. Not as good as the lawyer Recep has, Briefson, but Briefson calls on him when he wants another opinion. What do you think?"

"I guess there's no harm in calling him. But remember there are risks for us if we get involved."

"Risks?"

"Sure. A leak about us—naming us. Someone could kidnap us in plain daylight to get revenge for our involvement in..." Cristina didn't finish her statement and started to laugh as to imply it was just a joke. But she quickly realized it sounded more like a prophecy, and she remembered the blind man they had recently met. What had he predicted? Some bad omen. How eerie that experience had been!

"I should discuss this further with Eugen. He was hesitant about my helping Recep without having all the facts from other sources, apart from his wife. Eugen said the same thing you just did—involvement includes personal risk. He explained to me about hostage kidnapping and that Turkey hasn't proven to be a friendly country for cooperating. They don't abide by the U.N. resolution to prevent ransom payments from benefiting kidnapers. Hostage-taking has become a lucrative business in this country."

"I don't want to find out personally about ransoms. Better to keep it academic," Marina said.

"I've thought a lot about this," Cristina confessed. "And I asked Eugen what he thinks about my just turning the case over to a lawyer. No one would need to know I did it. Anonymously. And I can then placate my conscience that I'm helping Deniz and I'm doing what's right. Let the lawyers decide how to handle the case. And we're free of risks!"

"Speak to Eugen again. Maybe he or Petre know about some new developments. They might be privy to more information than what Deniz or Erol told us."

"It is right up their alley—political, criminal, international."

"Financial, too. Romania had a financial history with Iran and Turkey. Eugen and Petre were involved in that for years."

"They still are," Cristina stated. "I overheard them discussing how they're working in the Persian Gulf with Romania and the U.S. The two countries are partnering to protect the passageway of the Strait of Hormuz, in case Iran blocks tankers from entering or leaving. Iran has the largest border with the strait, and has the strongest presence there. 50% of the area's petrol passes through those waters, and 20% of the world's oil. Romania has recently become a close NATO ally with the U.S. and knows those waters."

"Sounds like high risk for Eugen and Petre."

"Eugen loves risk, but I don't. That's where we differ." Cristina paused, looked down, and then continued talking. "When we get to the square and sit at a café, I'll phone Eugen again. I'll speak Romanian. Best to keep the conversation secret if anyone is near."

Cristina and Marina walked toward the Blue Mosque, following the needle-like minarets. Dozens of men were lining up in the courtyard adjacent to the west gate to wash their hands and feet at the public fountain.

"Did you know," Marina asked, "that the worshippers in a mosque are all men? The Koran is written for men and assumes that women belong to a lower order of existence."

"Can women pray?"

"Of course, but it might be on the second floor of the Mosque. Or in the rear of the mosque–separated from the men."

"Was it always like that?" Cristina asked.

"Yes, until Ataturk became the leader and realized that a nation whose entire life is ruled only by the Koran could not progress in the modern world. He gave equal rights to women so they could go to school and work. He told them to remove their veils and be free."

"Amazing how the country has turned backwards," commented

Cristina. "Now women here seem to have fewer rights and less freedom than a hundred years ago."

"Yes, but a lot of people were unhappy that Ataturk wanted to adopt so many Western ways, like making laws about wearing Western-style hats instead of fezzes. I think it's important to honor tradition and one's own culture, too."

As Marina and Cristina chatted, they saw the gray stone domes of the Blue Mosque through chestnut trees. The large courtyard was filled with pigeons and with people trying to walk among the birds. Marina and Cristina entered through the north gate for non-worshipers and put on their head scarves. They looked at their watches and noticed that they had time to linger leisurely inside, as it was before the 90-minute closing to tourists to allow male followers to pray.

The main hall was immense, able to accommodate 25,000 worshippers at a time. The floor was covered with hundreds of carpets in different colors and sizes. The domed ceiling was lined with 20,000 blue ceramic tiles. Bright sun entered the stained glass windows and turned the mosque to shades of blue that made the interior appear as if it were part of heaven. The only noise came from the grandfather clocks given by Queen Victoria during the Crimean War, which struck the hour with inaccurate, British time.

Upon leaving the courtyard, Marina and Cristina continued to Eminonu port where there was a spice market. Cristina asked her friend, "Do you want to go inside and look for some new scents and creams?"

"No, not now. I'll go later with Tahquitz. He wants to introduce me to some merchant friends. Let's continue to Taksim Square."

They walked northward, crossing the Galata Bridge, taking note of the sun playing in and out while hinting of diamonds on the

Golden Horn. They passed several fruit stands, where carts were filled with pomegranates cut in half to display their ruby allure. A neighboring push-wagon was lined with rows of figs and apricots that created a pyramid of color. And as they continued strolling, the fruit stands were replaced by carts of kebabs displaying assortments of meats and fish. A white bearded man stood in front of a small grill, roasting ears of corn. Marina and Cristina were tempted, but continued on.

"I wonder if this neighborhood has an underground city like Tahquitz told us," Marina said.

"I read how residents of Istanbul have grown up with these archaeological ruins. Many of the caves haven't even been reported, because the owners of the buildings are afraid that disclosing the underground structures will lead to confiscating their properties."

"Some of the underground caves can extend below an entire neighborhood. Look at the café"—Marina pointed—"or the restaurant. Who knows what's underneath their floors? They've used the hidden caves and chambers since the 4th century to hide from their enemies, bury their dead, or even imprison the living."

Marina took her friend's arm, and they continued walking and chatting. "They probably use it today as a jail," she said.

"What a horrible thought," Cristina replied. "Do you think they have snakes underground? In Paris, they have rats, hordes of them, living in the Catacombs, surviving on the water and garbage. Maybe even snakes." Cristina squirmed and rubbed her nose, thinking of the smell and animals. "You have no idea, Marina, how much I hate snakes!"

They continued their stroll.

Scores of men were walking in the streets, and Marina eyed their mustaches as they passed by. "Did you ever see so many types of mustaches?" she asked. "It's as if they're parading their virility, using the hairs on their upper lip as a mating call."

"Not a bad idea.," Cristina, the artist, commented. "Our eye goes from the mustache to the lips and to a twinkle in their eye— tempting, challenging. Each with their own design." She laughed, thinking of the image.

They passed a residential street of tall, narrow houses with wrought-iron balconies. From the third floor of one, a woman yelled to a street vendor below. Marina and Cristina imagined she was asking, "What's fresh?" And he answered by pointing to arti- chokes, eggplant, and zucchini. She lowered a plastic bucket hanging from a rope and shouted what she wanted. He placed the order inside her bucket and she raised the rope, removed her goods, put some money in the bucket, and lowered it again to conclude their trade.

Marina and Cristina were content, enjoying the vibrancy of the city. They passed a group of young boys playing soccer between flower beds of red and pink tulips. In a corner, seated on a bench, were several old women dressed in black, chatting and enjoying each other's gossip. Cristina and Marina continued on, absorbing the city's mosaic of people, its fabric of culture and history, where time had stood still.

This was the calm side of Istanbul. The dangerous side was just around the corner.

# 19

*Istanbul, Turkey*
*November 27, 2017*

MARINA AND CRISTINA passed the metro station just in front of the
Taksim Republic Monument with its sculpted statues, including
one of Ataturk, the father of the Republic. Before them was
Taksim Gezi Park, a small green section, known for a brutal
demonstration against Ozogant's riot control police in 2013. The
protestors had wanted to stop the government's demolition of a
green park to build a shopping center. Thousands had fought
during the day, and then at night, they had set up tents to be ready
the next morning to demonstrate again when police, armed with
tear gas and pepper spray, set fire to the tents. But the protestors
weren't afraid—they spread to different cities to yell louder,
despite endless arrests.

Marina and Cristina approached Taksim Square and instantly
were bumped and pushed as thousands of protestors stormed
toward the center. These were demonstrators who were now
opposing Ozogant's recent arrests of nearly three thousand judges

and prosecutors, as well as hundreds of journalists, teachers, and ordinary citizens. Ozogant had imprisoned them without trials, accusing them of attempting a coup d'état to overthrow him and for being followers of his opponent, cleric Fettullah Gulen, who lived in the Poconos in Pennsylvania.

Crowds filled the square to protest. The multitude grew in passion, carrying placards with the words, "Ozogant = LIAR." Hundreds of heavily armed police surrounded the mob.

"I don't think we should stay here. It looks dangerous," Marina commented as she watched the police cordon off the area. She pointed to the café at the southeast corner where Tahquitz had said they should meet. "Let's go over there, away from the mob. Then we'll decide what to do."

"I'll ask what all this means and if we should leave," Cristina commented. They sat at a table outside, and Cristina flagged the waiter. "Do you speak English? *Parlez-vous français?*"

"Both. *Les deux,*" he answered, and automatically and handed them a menu.

"Not very friendly," commented Cristina. "He didn't give me a chance to ask if we should leave."

"Maybe he doesn't like foreigners. Seems we're the only women and non-Turks here." Marina was studying the faces of the demonstrators.

"I wonder who that strange man is following the waiter inside the cafe?" Cristina asked.

"Who? Where?"

"The weird one, dressed in black, short and muscular, with a knit bandana around his neck. Strange. Marina, are you sure this is the square and café where Tahquitz told us to meet him?"

"Yes, and it's the only café at this corner."

Cristina looked around and then commented, "A lot of bedlam going on. And it looks like it'll rain." She wasn't feeling comfortable.

Marina flagged the waiter. "We'll have two Turkish coffees, not sweet." She handed back the menus. "What's going on?" she asked him.

He left without answering.

"Should we stay?" Cristina shouted after him. He didn't answer. She turned to Marina. "It could get very dangerous."

"I'll call Tahquitz and ask him what we should do."

Marina took her phone and pressed his number. While waiting for his voice, she told Cristina, "Tahquitz installed a special app in my phone this morning before we left. It's a tracking device, and it's hooked up to his phone."

"Your Indian has a long history of tracking."

Marina smiled. "'My Indian?' That sounds a bit rude. There's no answer." She left a message: "We're at the café, southeast corner, just off the square. It's 1:30. We're going to leave. There's a big protest, and lots of police—it looks like trouble."

Just as she was finishing her message, the waiter approached them with their coffees and whispered, "Don't use your cell phones here. They're watching. You'll be noticed." He placed their coffees and the bill on the table and left.

Cristina stared at Marina. "It sounds like he knows something we don't, but that we should."

Marina took a sip of coffee. "Ick. Turkish coffee is certainly bitter." She reached for the sugar.

A policeman approached them. "Excuse me, ladies," he said in a heavily accented English.

Marina answered in a crisp, "Yes?"

"Wait a minute," he responded, faltering.

Cristina quickly grabbed a toothpick and put her phone under the table. She used the point of the toothpick to pop out the sim card, and slipped the card into her shoe.

Marina took her phone and buried it in her high boots. The soft leather folds of the boot hid the cell phone without a trace.

Another policeman came over to their table. "Good morning," he said in a clearer English. "What are you doing here? Are you taking photos?"

"No photos," answered Cristina. "I'm resting and enjoying your Turkish coffee. I'm a tourist. *Française. Parlez-vous...*"

"No. I speak English. You should leave now, but first, let me have your cell phone."

*"Je ne vous comprends pas,"* Cristina answered in French. *"Parlez-vous français?"*

He held out his hand, indicating she should give him her phone. Cristina stared at his empty hand.

"Don't move," he ordered and took out a radio. After a minute of quick Turkish verbiage, another man came to their table. He was dressed in a dark suit, white shirt, and tie. He stood out among the demonstrators of jeans-clad students and workers in blue overalls.

"My officer tells me you're not co-operating," he said to Cristina. "In Turkey, when a policeman says something, you listen. And he said you should leave and stop taking photos."

"I'm a tourist. I was using my phone to call my good friend, Deniz Akar, the singer, to ask her to join us at this café."

"Deniz Akar is a friend of yours?"

Marina tried hard not to smile. She was pleased with Cristina's cunning.

"Yes," Cristina answered. "In fact, didn't we meet the other night at her concert at her house? I'm sure I saw you there. All the VIP's of Istanbul were there."

"No. I heard about it, but I was on duty, working on our police fund raising."

"Oh? Fund raising?"

"Yes, to help the children."

"Like Deniz. Let me make the same donation that I made last night." Cristina dug into her bag and took out a $100 bill from a zippered compartment. "I hope this can help you... and the children."

He nodded slightly, took the bill, stuffed it in his pocket, and casually walked away.

Then Marina quickly put several bills on the table, hid her cell phone deeper in her boot, and said in Romanian, "Reception hasn't been good. Time to go."

"What about meeting Tahquitz? How is he going to find us?"

"I'll call him again and set up a safer meeting spot. I don't like it here. Something doesn't seem right."

They moved to walk away but were blocked by crowds of people entering Taksim Square from all corners. A young man bumped into Marina, and they both fell down. His large poster covered her. He picked it up, and before he could move away, Marina read the sign written in English, "Ozogant OUT! FREEDOM IN!"

Police ran after the protesters, preventing Marina and Cristina from leaving the square. They ducked into an empty alley for protection.

The demonstrators were shouting, "What do we want?"

"TRUTH!"

"What do we want?"

"TRUTH!"

Men in army uniforms took over the streets, knocking down people carrying signs. Tear gas filled the square. Security officers snapped heavy chains at protesters and pushed their way through the crowds. Some people dispersed, but most stayed, yelling louder, shouting "No!" until water hoses sprayed them down. Police on motorcycles stormed into the square and accelerated their speed as they targeted demonstrators. A group of students were hit. The ground turned bloody red.

More and more protestors filled the square. They yelled and shouted that they didn't want the government to close newspapers, close schools, or close courts. They were screaming, "FREE-DOM! JUSTICE! FREE US!"

They took posters and placards of Ozogant's face and threw them into bonfires until his smile was charred away.

A TV screen was set up in the center of the square and showed how police were clubbing everyone in their way. The screen focused on puddles of blood on the ground, sending a message throughout the world despite the government's blocking Facebook, Twitter, Instagram, and internet connections.

Marina and Cristina wanted to leave, but they couldn't. They were trapped in their alleyway. The police had cordoned off every street and angle of the square and were rounding up demonstrators. All the streets were blocked. They looked around, but found no exit.

Ten male students moved toward the center, each one holding a poster with the face of a dictator from history: Marx, Lenin, Stalin, Hitler, Mussolini, Gaddafi, Ceausescu, Saddam Hussein, and Mao. The last one was Ozogant.

The ten students made a circle in the middle of the square, while a group young women joined them and held flaming torches in their hands. One by one, each woman burned a poster with her torch and scorched the dictator away.

Ten other students walked into the center of the square, carrying posters with the words: "WE WANT JOBS!" Workers joined them and they all chanted, "DOWN WITH THE DICTA-TOR!" Police sprayed them with water cannons and hit them with bicycle chains.

Marina and Cristina still didn't know what to do. They were blocked, not able to move without being knocked down by the crowds or clobbered by the police.

They had lost their chance to leave.

# 20

*Istanbul, Turkey*
*November 27, 2017*

THE WEATHER CHANGED. Rain came down in torrents. The sky turned black. Strong winds blew posters around the square. Demonstrators ran away leaving the police without victims. Marina and Cristina were finally free to leave.

"What should we do?" Cristina asked.

"No taxis here."

"Should we wait until the rain is over?"

"We have no choice. I saw an overhead arch at that corner. Over there." Marina pointed. "We can stay there for a while and then return to the café to wait for Tahquitz."

"Wait. What's the matter with me? I can't walk. I feel dizzy."

"Me, too. Oh my god, I bet it was the coffee. Someone put something in our coffee."

"My eyes are blurry. I can't see," Cristina said.

"I feel faint. I'm falling…"

Marina woke up. Her eyes were covered with a tight cloth around her head. She couldn't see a thing. Her wrists and ankles were bound with rope, and she couldn't move. "Cristina? Cristina?"

"Huh?"

"Wake up! Are you okay?"

"Where are you? My eyes are blindfolded, and my legs and wrists are tied. Yours also?" Cristina's voice trembled.

"I don't know where we are or how we got here. We have to stay calm. We need to think what to do."

"Oh my God! What are we going to do? I'm so scared." Cristina started to cry.

"Let's figure out where we are. My fingers can touch the ground. It feels rocky, grainy. There's a thin layer of water about half an inch deep. It smells humid. And it's much warmer here than it was outside. We must be somewhere underground."

"It smells musty. It reminds me of the caves in Romania when we would go hiking when we were kids."

"Istanbul's subterranean caves. That's where we are. Listen. There are no sounds. No one else is here. Whoever brought us here has left us alone."

Cristina was sobbing. "We've been kidnapped. Our coffee was spiked with drugs—that was the bitter taste! That weird man following the waiter. The knit bandana around his neck must have been a face mask. He was watching us, and he put something in our coffee. The waiter warned us it was dangerous. We should have left. Why did we stay? Why?"

"Don't panic. Take a deep breath. Someone will come to save us. You must think positively."

"The kidnappers will be the ones to come to check on us. Do something to us—kill us! Oh my God, this is not possible. Why were we kidnapped? We're probably hostages. They must know you're rich. They're going to demand a huge ransom, I just know it."

"Don't be ridiculous. No one knows who I am here."

"Someone must know. You're tied up, and I'm tied up with you.""

"Get ahold of yourself! Tahquitz is supposed to meet us at the café. He'll realize something is wrong. He has the tracking app. They didn't find my phone. It's still in my boot. I feel it—it's still warm. Don't panic!"

"Should we yell? I'm surprised they didn't cover our mouths."

"No, don't yell. The kidnappers might be near and hear us. They probably know no one else can hear us anyway, so why bother gagging us too? Let's wait a while before we start screaming."

"We were the only women and foreigners in the area. We stood out." Cristina stopped talking. "Maybe it's something linked to hostage-diplomacy. It's becoming a sport in Turkey. There's that pastor and several other innocent Americans who were taken as hostages for ransom or as pawns to trade for Turkish political prisoners."

"But why us? We're just tourists."

"Maybe it's something other than being taken as hostages."

"What do you mean?"

"Why did Tahquitz put a tracking app in your phone this morning? That doesn't seem like a coincidence. What kind of device is it?" Cristina's suspicion crept into her voice.

"He's into all kinds of technical gadgets. It's his hobby. He told me if I ever got into trouble, this new app could come in handy. He thought the device might also be connected to the American government's internet-based network. Something the Americans have been experimenting with—called Covcom. He asked me for my cell phone to install it. I figured why not?"

"Does Tahquitz work for the C.I.A., do you think? Is that why he had the device? Maybe that's why they kidnapped you. And me too, just for being with you. We've been seen with him—at Deniz's. Maybe we were seen on TV with her. They might have followed us to Erol's house—or maybe it has something to do with his mysterious sister and brother-in-law. Who are they? What do they do to have such a beautiful home? They're never home."

"You're spinning into panic mode. Let's calm down and think of how we can get away from here."

"It sounds like what you have in your boot could be a system only used by American intelligence or C.I.A. operatives."

"You read too many spy novels."

"Do you think there are snakes here? I'm so afraid of snakes. At least I can't see them, but I'd be able to feel them. And they'd be able to feel me. I hate them."

"Just calm down. There aren't any snakes here."

Cristina took a deep breath. "I'm hungry and thirsty. We didn't eat any lunch. Just that damned coffee! What are we going to do? I don't know how long I can last."

"I don't think we've been here that long. And we'll last as long as we have to. Just don't panic."

Cristina started to sob hysterically.

Marina felt sorry for her. "Please don't cry. We have to stay strong."

"Let's keep talking," Cristina suggested, "or I'll go crazy. If I have to die, I'm glad I'm with you, Marina. You're the person I know the longest. My dearest friend."

"You won't die here—nor will I."

"Suddenly I feel religious. Should we make our last confession to each other?"

"No! We're not going to die here. I've just fallen in love after so many years."

"Ah, love. Let's talk about love. That will change our thoughts,"

Cristina said. "No, better yet, let's talk about sex. My turn. My first time wasn't as pleasant as yours, but it will distract me."

"Okay, Talk about sex."

"Well," Cristina hesitated. "Unlike yours… it wasn't of my own initiative."

"Tell me. It'll get your mind off the present."

"Okay. I was eighteen, the September of beginning art school at the university in Cluj. You remember how I wore my red hair long and straight down to my waist?"

Cristina took a deep breath. More breaths; deeper. She tried to stay in control and concentrate on her story. Not to think of where she was. "I'm so scared."

"No, you're not," Marina said. "You're brave and you were telling me a story when you were young and very beautiful, and you were already designing your own clothes. Beginning a brilliant career."

"Yes, I loved design." Cristina tried to focus on her story. "But there was a problem in our fashion class. We were ten students and had only three sewing machines. We all had to wait our turn. Some of the students didn't like that, but I didn't mind because while I waited, I designed my own clothes and sewed them by hand. Actually, I liked sewing that way, so I could control each stitch."

Cristina paused. "Continue," Marina said.

"Okay. So, our professor was a well-known fashion designer. He was eager to teach us and encouraged our creativity—when he was sober. But often, he'd come to class drunk, very drunk, hardly able to lecture. He'd say to the women, 'Whoever lets me kiss them can use the sewing machine first.'"

"How awful. Were there any women who actually kissed him?"

"Yes! I stayed away. I wasn't in a rush to use the machines."

"What a pig," Marina said.

"One day, he was more drunk than usual, hardly able to stand or walk. He came over to me, pulled the fabric I was cutting out of my hand, and said, 'You, Cristina, don't you want the sewing machine?'"

"I said, 'No, I'm happy sewing by hand. I'll wait my turn. 'But I want a kiss from you!' he yelled. I looked around the room for a male colleague who could defend me, but no one was in the room. I had been so engrossed with cutting my samples that I hadn't realized the class was over and everyone had left."

"Oh, Lord. I don't like where this is going," said Marina.

"He grabbed my hair, pulled me off my chair, and moved on top of me, yelling, 'I want a kiss!' He opened his belt and lowered his pants. Pointing to his underwear, he said, 'Here. I want a kiss here.' I yelled, 'No! Stop!' I pointed the scissors I still had in my hands towards his stomach, ready to plunge them into his bloated belly. He was afraid of me and moved away. I dropped the scissors and ran out of the room."

"Did you report him?"

"No. No. I didn't want a scandal, and I was worried what it would me for my future. He was too famous. I just didn't return to his class, which was a double injustice because I was just discovering my passion for fashion design."

"How sad. My poor Cristina. I'm so sorry for you."

"I thought that was the end of him, but no. One day, I needed some fabric for a design. Students were allowed to choose any fabric they wanted from a section in a storage area located in the basement of the design building. It was dark there—only one 40-watt light bulb. The students would use a flashlight that was kept at the door and I took it.

"No one was in the room. I started rummaging through the boxes looking for fabric when I heard some footsteps. I turned around and saw him. He smelled of vodka and was shouting some gibberish that I couldn't understand.

"I raised the flashlight to warn him I'd strike him with it if he came closer. 'Get away!' I yelled. I ran to the door. He ran after me, grabbed me, took the flashlight from my hand, and hit me on the head with it."

"Oh, no!"

"Fortunately, because he was drunk, he didn't really hit me hard. I got away from him again, but I still panic every time I think about what could have happened." Cristina started to sob. "I got home, but I was in a daze. How, I don't remember... I had never seen my parents cry before."

"What did they do?"

"My father took my case to the communist leader of our district. The bad luck was that the leader knew the professor, who gave Christmas presents of his fashions to important women. The leader's wife was on the professor's Christmas list.

"It was useless. The communist boss of the region counter-attacked by saying it was my fault—that I led the professor on—teased him. In other words, I asked for it." Cristina couldn't stop sobbing.

"There was no justice in that country," Marina said. "Bribes made the law. Bribes and lies."

"Wait. Let me finish the story. Maybe God renders justice." Cristina took a few deep breaths.

"Several months later, I saw him again. He was in the middle of the school garden. It was a sunny afternoon, and dozens of students were surrounding him. I stayed far in the back, away from his sight, but I didn't leave because I was so curious."

"What was he doing?"

"He had a viper wrapped around his neck. He told the crowd it was his pet. The snake was about nine feet long, very heavy, and had a long slithery tongue that kept shooting out.

"The professor was drunk, and he was sticking out his tongue to catch the viper's tongue. It looked like they were tongue-kissing. Then the professor took off his shirt, exposed his chest, and had the snake lick his breasts and then his belly button.

"All the students were clapping and yelling, 'More! More! More!' The professor was now out of control. So was the snake. They kept tongue-kissing. The snake's tongue licked him… and then it happened!"

"What happened?" Marina gasped.

"The roar of laughter from the students got louder and louder. They were stomping their feet, yelling, 'More! More!' Their noise was deafening. The snake went wild. Acid from his tongue squirted out, spraying the professor's face with its deadly venom. The professor fell to the ground. The snake freed itself from his hands and moved to the circle of students, and with its long slithery tongue started to spray at everyone. Someone called security. Guards ran over and tried to catch the snake. But they couldn't, and finally one of the guards shot the snake dead."

"And the professor?"

"The guards arrested him. Put him in a straitjacket and sent him to a psychiatric hospital. You can imagine what they did to him there. No one ever saw him again."

"Wow! What a story."

"Now you know why I hate snakes so much. I associate them with that loathsome professor." Cristina stopped talking and breathed hard.

"It sounds to me like you ought to appreciate snakes and how they can do your bidding for you."

"Ha," Cristina said. "Maybe so. But, it took me several years to trust a man after that. In Paris, I met Eugen. I want to believe that Eugen was my first and only man."

"Cristina, my dear friend. I am so sorry for what happened to you."

"No, don't feel sorry. Maybe the awful things that happen to us teach us a lesson. It made me realize that sex needs love and how much I appreciate Eugen."

"You never told me about this."

"You were in Bucharest working with Dr. Aslan and Stefan. We didn't see each other again until we both went to Germany with Mica's help and we were busy negotiating with her lawyers."

"Yes, other challenges."

---

Marina and Cristina tried not to cry. They were hungry and thirsty. Although they had been kidnapped, they had each other, and they were opening their hearts to each other like they had done when they were teenagers.

"If we stay here, if we're held captive any longer, we can discuss love. Pure love—separate from sex. That would be nice." Marina was trying to distract her friend, calm her, but then suddenly, Marina stopped talking.

"Wait! Cristina, I feel my phone vibrating. Maybe it's a message. Tahquitz must be trying to reach me."

"It's the app," Cristina whispered. "Oh God, please, please God, help us."

"Listen. I hear footsteps—lots of them."

"The kidnappers—maybe they're back, along with some others. They'll attack us! Oh my God! Help us!"

"Shh, don't talk," Marina warned. "I smell something. Candles. Eucalyptus. Tahquitz had those in his bathroom for emergencies when there's no light."

"Marina." A whisper of her name. "It's me. Don't be afraid. I've brought help."

She smelled the candles as the speaker came closer. Then Tahquitz untied the band on her eyes, freed her hands, her legs. Another man did the same for Cristina. It was the architect,

Cemele, whom they had met at Deniz's concert. Cemele, who was Istanbul's underground expert. The two women sobbed with relief.

"Here's some water." Tahquitz gave Marina and Cristina his canteen.

A policeman placed them on stretchers and took them out to a waiting helicopter.

## 21

*American Hospital in Istanbul*
*November 28, 2017*

MARINA SAT up as the helicopter was landing on the roof of the American hospital in Istanbul. Tahquitz was seated next to her, holding her hand.

"Thank you so much," she whispered. Then she asked him, "Is Cristina okay?"

"Yes, she'll be fine. You two have been through a lot, though. Just rest."

Marina turned to the stretcher next to her. "Cristina, are you okay? How are you?"

"I'm all right."

"Let me give you both some more water," Tahquitz offered, as two paramedics came to take the stretchers out of the helicopter. He explained to Marina and Cristina that the hospital where they were going had a helicopter pad on the roof.

"Cemele thought that it would be best if you stayed at the

American hospital for a day or two until you feel stronger," Tahquitz said, without going into details.

"We'll feel better after a meal and a rest. What do you think, Cristina?"

"For sure," she mumbled.

"The nurses will serve you whatever you want. The doctors on staff are very well trained. The equipment is modern and highly specialized, if needed."

"Cemele, Tahquitz, I am so thankful to you both," said Cristina.

As they came over to her stretcher, she kissed each one's hand and whispered, "God bless you."

---

Marina and Cristina shared a large room overlooking the hospital's garden. Cemele was busy instructing the nurses to take special care. Tahquitz was seated in the middle of the two beds, answering their questions.

"When did you realize we were in danger?" Marina asked.

"It must have been at the moment when you were kidnapped, just before the rain started. I tried to call you to suggest we meet at another café away from the square. I had heard about the demonstration, and I was worried. When you didn't answer, I turned on the app."

"What a genius you are," Marina said, smiling. "How did you have such foresight to think of installing a tracking system on my cell phone?"

"Pure luck."

"No, not a coincidence. There is a God," Cristina said.

"I could see you were moving underground. I called Cemele immediately and asked him if he had blueprints for the caves under Taksim Square. He said he could locate them in a few minutes and that a I should meet him at his office. He was already prepared with candles, flashlights, rubber boots, canteens, emergency backpacks of medical supplies, and special glasses to see in the dark. He even took a gun and handed me one.

"We left with dozens of blueprints and our backpacks filled with supplies. I was concerned that the passageways would be blocked or inundated with water."

"Did the blueprints show some kind of opening where you could enter and find us?"

"Yes, but to locate you, we had to travel more than four miles underground. We practically ran all the way."

"Weren't you concerned the kidnappers were still there or nearby?" Cristina asked.

"Yes," Cemele answered. "That's why, before we left, I contacted the police chief of a special kidnapping division of the best-trained officers. Six of them followed us underground. They were armed, and two carried the stretchers."

"Were there any kidnappers in the vicinity or near us?" Cristina asked.

"Yes. Two, who were guarding the exit of the cave." Tahquitz looked down.

"What happened?" Cristina asked, raising her voice.

"Two policemen shot them in the legs," Cemele answered. "They were identified as being part of a kidnapping ring targeting tourists and demanding ransoms."

"Oh my God," moaned Cristina.

"The chief also had a back-up team of police in case there were more criminals," Tahquitz explained. "But there weren't. Your kidnappers must have realized we were on their trail. They abandoned you and ran for their lives."

"The police cordoned off the square," Cemele said, "to block all cars and pedestrians in the Taksim area and to be ready in case they return. Police were guarding every corner and the adjacent streets."

"Oh my God," Marina whispered. "I feel so guilty to get the police involved like that for us."

Cristina sighed, nodded her head, and looked for her cell phone. Not able to find it, she asked, "Can someone lend me their phone? I want to call my husband."

Tahquitz passed her his. She quickly sent a text message to Eugen. Everyone was quiet while her fingers moved rapidly. A nurse came in with an assortment of food on trays, and an aide propped up their beds so they could eat comfortably.

"Tell me more," Marina said to Tahquitz. "I realize how dangerous this rescue operation was. You both risked your lives for us. We can never thank you enough."

"We should make a contribution to the police unit," Cristina insisted, returning the cell phone to Tahquitz.

"Of course," Marina agreed. "To all the divisions involved."

"No need," Cemele insisted. "Everyone is satisfied that you're safe. They're proud of their work."

"We insist," Marina said. "But for the moment, please, tell us more.'

"I was very concerned throughout the operation," Tahquitz confessed. "I kept wondering if I should contact someone in the Turkish government. You're an American citizen, Marina, and you, Cristina, French. I thought about calling your consulates. The possibility of your being kidnapped for a ransom was foremost in my mind. I was thinking about how to handle that. Should I wait until someone contacts me about paying money? I was also worried about a recent trend of hostage diplomacy–to trade you for Turkish hostages. I didn't know what to do, or what would transpire, so I decided to put the case into the hands of the police chief, who I know well."

"We discussed the different options of how to proceed," Cemele concurred.

"What about the helicopter? Why did you use that and not an ambulance?"

"Good question." Tahquitz squeezed Marina's hand. "We were afraid that more kidnappers were somewhere near, watching us. They could have had their own tracking device. We were working against the clock. A helicopter would allow us a quicker exit."

"Are such helicopters common in Istanbul?" Cristina asked. "It looked like it had been gutted out to fit in two stretchers."

"The police had to search their computer system for such a chopper. It had to also be equipped medically." Tahquitz lowered his head and wiped tears from his cheeks. "We didn't know what shape you'd be in." It was the doctor in him who was speaking.

## 22

*Istanbul, Turkey*
*November 29, 2017*

MARINA AND CRISTINA walked out of the hospital, still feeling the emotional upheaval of their kidnapping, but relieved that they were safe. Tahquitz wanted to escort them back to his house or send a driver to pick them up, but Marina and Cristina insisted that they wanted to walk to his place, just the two of them, and enjoy their freedom.

It was a chilly November morning, but the sun was out and shining brightly. The fog that had surrounded the city had lifted and the winds were calm. Marina and Cristina were feeling the joy of chatting together—two dear friends.

The previous day of horror was behind them, and they tried to think of it as a bad experience from the past. They were grateful that they hadn't been harmed. Their concern for each other during the ordeal had made their bond even stronger.

"It's amazing how our kidnappers were able to get us underground into a cave and we didn't feel anything or remember anything."

"There must have been some powerful drugs in that coffee. I still feel a little queasy."

"The chief of police has assured us that they're looking to see if there are more kidnappers who are part of the ring."

"What a horrible experience."

"For sure. Let's try to forget it," Marina said. "The most important thing is that we are walking now, free, safe, and appreciating it."

"I'd like to do something for Cemele and Tahquitz to show our gratitude," Cristina said. "What do you think of giving them a party? We can celebrate them as heroes for saving our lives."

"I like that idea. I could use a social event, too, to try to take my mind off this whole ordeal."

"How about in Paris as my guests? Do you think they'd like that?"

Just as they were discussing the details of when and where, Cristina heard someone yelling her name.

"Cristina! Cristina!"

It was a man's voice–Eugen's. Where was he? She waved her hands in the air. She took her bag and swung it high. "Here! Eugen!"

In a second, he was there, next to her, holding her tight in his arms.

"It's not possible!" Cristina, said, kissing him. "I can't believe it. What are you doing in Istanbul?"

"I didn't want to tell you when you left Paris, but I knew then that I was being sent to Turkey. You called me at first two days ago, and again, today, from Tahquitz's cell phone. I called him back and he told me what had happened. Are you okay?" He took her face in his hands, studied her tired eyes, and whispered, "My love, if any harm had come to you, I don't know what I'd do."

"I'm fine. We're both fine."

He held her tight. "I've spoken to the chief of police. I offered to give him a few of my men to assist in the investigation. But he said he has two units of police working on the case."

He took her hand and kissed it, and then her cheeks. "I promise to stay in touch with him until this is solved. I'm also looking into the motive behind your kidnapping. I don't think hostage diplomacy should become as common as stealing a tourist's wallet. Anywhere!"

He turned to Marina and asked her, "Are you okay?"

"Yes. We have not been harmed in *any way*." She smiled to reassure him. "Not Cristina, not me. Just shaken up."

"I understand," he said, hugging Marina and kissing Cristina again. "Please tell me everything that happened."

"Eugen, my love, I'll tell you everything later, but please tell me first, where were you a few days ago? I tried calling you several times. I was so worried about you."

"I'm sorry I couldn't tell you, and that I was incommunicado. This has been top secret. No one but Petre and I could know." He looked down as a way to apologize and remained silent for a beat.

"But now that the operation is over, I can tell you," he confessed. "We were sent first to Bucharest to be briefed and do some work there. Then we went to the Gulf of Oman, representing Romania and the U.S."

He took Christina's and Marina's hands and walked them over to a quiet spot behind several trees. "No one is to know this. Top secret."

They raised their hands to swear.

"Petre and I are creating a new diplomatic opening with Iran for the C.I.A. Peace and security in the Middle East and Persian Gulf are extremely important for both the U.S. and Iran.

"Romania will thread the needle between the two countries because of their ties in the region."

"You mean you're finally going to learn to sew?" Cristina teased him.

"Sew? We hope to sow benefits for the U.S. and region."

"Ha ha," Marina said. "Like Ariadne with a thread and sword to help Theseus escape the labyrinth. I know something about that. Am I Ariadne or Theseus?"

They all laughed.

"Petre and I will help broker Romania with the U.S. and Iran. We'll serve as a go-between as we've done in the past. Romania has good diplomatic relations with both countries, and no country involved wants to draw attention to negotiations until there's something concrete to show."

"And how will you do that?" Christina asked.

"We're preparing to dispatch a submarine with the official explanation of patrolling piracy in the Arabian Sea. But secretly, the submarine will be the meeting place for diplomacy. We're not going to the Strait of Hormuz, which is too obvious, but nearby, to the Gulf of Oman."

"You mean the Americans and Iranians will conduct diplomacy under sea in a submarine?" Marina asked, astonished.

"Yes. The press won't find them fathoms away." He smiled and then continued.

"Petre and I had to register the American submarine to a Romanian shipping company. We did that in Bucharest. And since we were in the neighborhood," Eugen said, "we continued on to Istanbul to investigate the gas-for-gold scandal that Iran has been involved in." Then he gave Cristina his cryptic smile. "Maybe Romania, as well."

"What do you mean?" she asked.

He laughed. "It was because of you. You became so obsessed with Recep Sharatt that it waas contagious. I started to research why you were so interested in him, and then I understood. When you returned home from your first visit from Istanbul and showed me the photos of Ozogant's son and son-in-law that you had from Deniz, I dug deeper into the matter. My research confirmed what you said about Ozogant Junior working with rebel organizations was true."

"Don't forget," Marina reminded him, "what Deniz told us about his being involved in transporting oil for the Kurds. Imagine that!"

"I see a pattern," Cristina said, assessing the situation. She was so happy to see Eugen and to forget her horrible ordeal that she threw all her energy back into the gas-for-gold case.

"I've been thinking of all the characters that are part of this story and how they're interconnected," she said.

"On the top is an older generation with Rafsanjani, Khorasami, and Rustany pulling the strings for their marionettes who are the young men–Recep Sharatt, Balal Zanssany, Belcan Ozogant, who are entitled sons that prefer crime to work. Reminds me of my love for Russian literature and Turgenev's *Fathers and Sons*. Fathers made the contacts, and sons benefited. And they kept the money in the family. Power sharing."

"You're right," and Eugen kissed his wife. "Not only are you beautiful and talented, but you're smart, too." He took her in his arms. "My dear Cristina, I hope you didn't suffer too much. I love you so much."

"It made me stronger–stronger to love you." She poked him playfully in his stomach and started to laugh.

"Because I love you so much," Eugen said, "and you asked me to help Deniz with Recep, I took your cues and convinced Petre that this case deserved a visit to incredible Istanbul to see what we could do."

"Incredible, yes." Both Marina and Cristina tried to laugh, but the memory of their horrendous experience would not entirely disappear, no matter how hard they tried.

"Where's Petre?" Marina asked.

"He's been canvassing the area around Taksim Square. He's looking to see if he can find anything related to your being kidnapped. He's questioning the people at the café and even exploring the underground cave where you were held. Let me phone him that I've found you."

Eugen took out a miniature two-way radio that looked like an ordinary cigarette lighter and spoke in Romanian, telling Petre to join them and giving directions where they were.

"Why are you *really* in Istanbul?" Cristina asked again, smiling. "And when you were in Bucharest, did they brief you also on any other matters?"

"You are too smart, my love." He laughed.

"I know you have a better reason than just following-up what I told you about Deniz and Recep."

"Yes, tell us why you and Petre are really here," Marina persisted.

"We need proof."

"Proof about what?"

"Proof against Ozogant. Proof he's involved in the gas-for-gold scheme. Proof he partnered willingly with Iran. Proof he's selling arms to ISIS. Proof that the gold was originally Ceausescu's."

Cristina laughed. "Ceausescu's gold! Seems we're on the same treasure hunt!"

Eugen's walkie-talkie buzzed. He answered, spoke to Petre, and told Cristina and Marina that they'll meet Petre at the Ciargan Palace Hotel, where they were staying.

As they walked, following the Bosphorus, Eugen explained another reason he and Petre were in Turkey.

"We're here also coordinating one hundred of our best men from different divisions—C.I.A., F.B.I., the Navy Seals, Special Operations Forces...."

"Why in Istanbul?" Marina interrupted him.

"We want to do what we did in 1989 in Timisoara and then

Bucharest. Start pandemonium in one city—Istanbul—and then the capital, Ankara. See where the chaos takes us. Bring in more men if needed."

"Do you have a long-term plan of action?"

"That will come from the Turkish people. They'll help us decide the next step. We'll see how much they really want democracy. Sharatt's and Akan's trial yesterday in New York was blocked on Turkish TV and on the Turkish internet, but the students were able to circumvent the block and make the trial public on a cable streaming channel. They transmitted the segment when Sharatt testified that Ozogant approved and allowed the gas-for-gold scheme. You saw at Taksim Square how the students were demonstrating against Ozogant. They want him out."

"Yes, but will they really be able to do anything?" asked Cristina.

"Maybe. U.S. Intelligence is involved. They hope to direct the students' fury to an end goal. We'll encourage the people's anger against Ozogant now that the facts of the gas-for-gold scheme have been televised from the New York trial. It's a little Machiavellian," Eugen said. "Our end justifies their means."

"I guess I don't fully understand," Cristina remarked.

"We want the end to take us to the beginning—to the gold. We want to understand the cycle—learn whose gold was used for the scheme. Did the Turks begin their operation with Ceausescu's gold? Did the Iranians transfer the gold to Turkey so Turkey could jump-start the scheme, recycle the gold, and send it back to Iran? Was the gold being kept warm by Iran's Rafsanjani until someone could launder it out?"

"You mean Sharatt?"

"Yes, and his friends, with Zanssany's brain working behind the scene." Eugen hesitated and smiled at his wife.

"Being that I love you so much and I'm happy you're safe, I have a present for you."

"What?" she asked curiously.

"I downloaded the vlog from Finland that you've been following. They posted it on YouTube, that trial-segment when Recep serves as a witness against his colleague—Mohamet Hakan Akan, deputy C.E.O. of Hachebanque, the facilitating bank of the gas-for-gold scandal. Recep made a deal with the U.S. government to enter the American Witness Protection program. He gave a lot of information. More than what has been made public. Let me show you why the Turkish people are furious about Ozogant."

Eugen took out his phone and turned on the video.

## 23

*Vlog from the trial of Mohamet Hakan Akan*
*U.S. District Courthouse, Brooklyn, New York*
*November 29, 2017*

*Viewers, before we transmit to you a video segment from the trial of Mohamet Hakan Akan from Brooklyn, New York, we'd like to first give you our comments and some background information:*

*The timing was right for Recep Sharatt's genius to find a creative path to survive. He was miserable in prison. He reported that his cellmate from the Ivory Coast was assaulting him. The African defended himself by claiming that it was Recep who had assaulted him, not he who assaulted Recep. The victim demanded an apology. So Recep deposited money into the African's bank account even though he protested the stories were fake. And afterwards, Recep continued doing what he knew best—he asked a friend in Turkey to deposit $45,000 in a guard's checking account for getting him a bottle of scotch and some cigarettes.*

*It was at this time that Special Counsel Robert Miller was investigating General Ike Flemm for his role in helping the president's relationship with Russia. Bob Miller found out that General Flemm also* had Turkish friends in high places who had paid him a $530,000 consulting fee for some favors. The Turkish government offered the General an additional $15 million to get Recep Sharatt kidnapped or extradited somehow, and out of jail. He declined, but certainly, this was a signal to the Special Counsel that Recep Sharatt might be worthy of more attention.

Sharatt did not deny that he was ready to make a deal—he would have told the Americans anything to get out of prison. And his team of lawyers was busy working to make possible a plea bargain with the American government—Sharatt's information for the Witness Protection Program.

The bad luck of the deal was for Akan, deputy C.E.O. of Turkey's facilitator-bank in the laundering scheme. He was also in a Manhattan prison, but the Judge did not accept his offer to pay $50 million for bail to stay in a luxurious Manhattan apartment rather than in a cell. Unfortunately, Akan didn't have Ben Briefson or his equal for legal representation. And his friend, Sharatt, was ready to point his finger at him, and even include the president of Turkey as accomplice in the scheme. The only thing Sharatt had in mind was how quickly he could be set free, not to Turkey but perhaps to somewhere sunny, maybe Miami or even Dubai, where his shell companies might be secretly holding millions for him. Sharatt was missing his jet-set style of life.

When Sharatt was questioned about his loyalty to Akan, his former co-worker, he shrugged his shoulders and raised his eyes upward. Sharatt was an ardent believer that God helps those who help themselves.

We now take you directly to the trial of Mohamet Hakan Akan, live streaming, with Recep Sharatt as star witness. Sharatt has acknowledged that he has flipped to help the Americans—and also to help himself. He has shaved his beard, looks trim from his jail-diet, and is dressed stylishly in a navy blazer, white shirt, and red tie.

For our international viewers who may not follow all the English of the trial, we have put below the corresponding English captions.

Sharatt asked for a smartboard and diagrammed from the stand the *details of his scheme. As he moved from point A to point B, he explained the complex design step by step. He spoke confidently like a business professor giving a lecture to students about white collar crime. He used spreadsheets that were colored-coded and posters that he had prepared to document the long list of accomplices with corresponding amounts of kickbacks and gifts. He explained precisely what the jury wanted to hear. But he omitted some slight details because no one asked him:*

*Why did the Iranian government believe he was holding his best friend's billions of dollars?*

*How much did Balal Zanssany actually owe the Iranian petrol ministry?*

*What did Belcan Ozogant, son of Turkey's president, do as part of the scheme? What about the son-in-law?*

*And what about Iranian Akbar Rafsanjani?*

*Within hours, Recep's explanations, diagrams, posters, and spreadsheets made their way secretly through Turkey's internet to Ankara's cafés. They also surfaced on the front pages of Istanbul's newspapers and dominated Turkish TV screens. An angry Ozogant swore revenge. He lashed out against the snitch and defended his executive powers by claiming, 'We bought natural gas from a country we have an agreement with so our citizens wouldn't be cold in winter.'*

*Ozogant refuted Sharatt's accusations that he was complicit in facilitating Turkish banks and companies like Twopratts to move $5-10 million per day to shell and proxy companies around the world, especially to Malta and the U.S.*

*Ozogant, instead, decreed that Recep had committed crimes as a Turkish citizen and 'leaked state secrets like a rat!' As punishment, the Turkish government had no choice but to seize all Recep's properties, including his homes, his planes, his race horses, yachts, sports cars, even his gold-plated pistol. They went after his father, his brother, his wife, even his daughter—and stripped them of their properties and treasures.*

*Recep was worried. He had worked very hard to amass his fortune, and now had lost everything. Was he right to have made a plea bargain and trade information for freedom? To get an answer, he contacted his mystic to ask what would be the outcome of his cooperating with the American prosecutors.*

*The fortune teller prophesized, 'Wrong choices made for the wrong reasons. The American government may not protect you. You may have to tell more.'*

---

*We now continue our transmission of live-streaming from Helsinki, Finland, with the actual trial of Mohamet Hakan Akan that also contains our embedded comments of his interrogation.*

*We are filming the appearance of witness Recep Sharrat at this trial, who is being interrogated by chief prosecutor, Ms. Jung Joo Park, of the U.S. Attorney's Office for the Southern District of New York.*

*Recep Sharatt is taking the stand as a participant of the American Government's Witness Protection Agency:*

*"Mr. Sharatt." Ms. Park approached the stand. "You are now working for us. So we are eager for you to make clear to the Court the workings of this gas-for-gold scheme. To achieve our objective, I will begin by asking you a few questions that may initially seem unrelated to our case. But please, answer everything and allow me to proceed step by step to clarify my reasoning.*

*"Mr. Sharatt, you say you earned $150 million dollars for your work from 2010-2017. Some reports I've read claim that number is modest compared to the actual amount. Whatever it is, we're talking about more money than all my colleagues from the D.A.'s office have earned together from their salaries."*

*Laughter filled the room.*

*"Did you ever do anything for Turkey or Iran in philanthropy to help those less fortunate than yourself? Anything to thank the countries that gave you such an opportunity to accumulate so much wealth at such a young age?"*

"Yes. For Turkey, I donated $4.5 million to Mrs. Alara Ozogant's education charity, TOGEM, to assist the mentally and physically disabled."

"Was there a celebration to thank you?"

"Yes, on April 21, 2015. Mrs. Ozogant and the President came to an award ceremony for me. They appreciated my gift."

"Did you make any other financial contributions?"

"Yes, in June 2015, I helped Turkey raise their export quota, due to all my creative trade activities. For that, I received the Top Exporter Award from the Turkish Exporters Assembly."

"The press called you Ozogant's Goldfinger."

Laughter. Judge Friedman banged his gavel.

"Silence in the courtroom. Please continue, Ms. Park."

"What about Iran? You were born there."

"Yes. I have equal loyalty to both countries."

"Can you explain to the court how you expressed your gratitude to Iran."

"I've volunteered my time to create a high-tech center in a university."

"Where is this university?"

"In Rafsanjan, a district in south central Iran, about six hundred kilometers from Tehran. The tech center will be part of Rafsanjan University of Medical Sciences."

"Why there and not in Tehran? Or another city in Iran?"

"I was asked to build it there."

"I see. By whom?"

"An Iranian friend."

"Please tell the court who this friend is."

He looked down, cleared his throat, and muttered, "Balal Zanssany."

There was a murmur throughout the room. Judge Friedman banged his gavel several times. "Order in the court! Please continue."

"If I'm not mistaken, Mr. Zanssany is presently in Evin Prison in

Tehran, sentenced to death by hanging, for crimes to the earth...That's what his sentence says."

Recep rubbed his hands together, obviously uncomfortable.

"Can you tell us why Mr. Zanssany is interested in this project? Doesn't he have more important things to worry about?"

"This project dates back to seven years ago. Mr. Zanssany told me about a senior person in Iran who wanted to have centralized several tech companies in one location at the medical school. Mr. Zanssany didn't know how to go about getting the land. So he asked me to help. I was able to buy fifteen hectares—about forty acres. Construction started several years ago."

"Who is this senior person?"

"I forgot."

"If I said the name, would that stimulate your memory? Mr. Sharatt, I must remind you that you are under oath. In the U.S. if you lie, it is considered perjury, which is a criminal offense. It is hard to get immunity if you are convicted of perjury."

He coughed, cleared his throat, and said looking down, "Maybe if you said his name that would help me remember."

"Let me guess. My research tells me that the section of Rafsanjan that you have mentioned, is known for pistachio farms. An important export for Iran. Millions of dollars per year, maybe billions. Does the name Rafsanjani from Rafsanjan ring a bell?"

"Yes, now I recall, that's the person."

"He died last year—January 8, 2017. At the time, he was considered the richest man in Iran, owning most of the pistachio farms as well as high tech companies, tech start-ups, copper mines, oil fields, hotels, airlines—should I go on?" She was almost out of breath from the list. Ms. Park turned to the judge. "Rafsanjani's opponents have questioned the initial source of his money for investment use. They claim corruption." She paused and stared at Sharatt, and then continued.

"What is the budget for this project? You must know. You have *illustrated to the court your astuteness with numbers, spreadsheets, and kickback diagrams."*

*"$100-150 million."*

*"Again... that's a lot of money. Who's paying? And why?"*

*"Objection, Your Honor!" yelled an attorney from the opposing side.*

*"Ms. Park, what are you getting at?" Judge Friedman asked her.*

*"Your Honor, I've researched this case thoroughly. I've spent many nights and weekends in the office, reading and studying. I have some findings that I'd like to share with you and the jury."*

*"Continue."*

*"Rafsanjani is the founder of the Islamic Azad University that has thirty-five campuses spread out in several countries. The main campus, which also houses the medical school, is in Rafsanjan, where he was born. The university has more than 1,700,000 students in total and is the largest private university in the world! It's estimated to be valued at $20-25 billion."*

*There was complete silence in the courtroom.*

*"Rafsanjani is no longer here to tell us how he became so rich, but I believe he was the leader of the gas-for-gold scheme, and he used gold that he stored in a private bank to assist him in his start ups and business investments."*

*Noise in the courtroom drowned out Ms. Park's last words.*

*"Order in the court!" Judge Friedman shouted. "We will recess for lunch and resume in one hour." He banged his gavel, moved to Ms. Park, and whispered, "I will see you privately in my chambers."*

*She turned her back to the judge. She hadn't finished her cross examination.*

*"Members of the jury, please do not leave. Let me continue. Rafsanjani's gold came from Ceausescu in December 1989, who deprived twenty-four million Romanians of a decent life. I know about this from my father-in-law. My husband is Romanian. His father escaped Romania in 1970 after being arrested and tortured! He suffered his entire life from what they did to him in prison."*

"Objection! Objection!" came the voices of several lawyers. "No personal motives allowed in the court! Objectivity is the rule of law!"

"Silence! Order!" Judge Friedman shouted as he banged his gavel. "Ms. Park, I have called for a recess and for you to come with me."

A journalist blocked her from leaving. He took out his phone and snapped a photo as tears poured down her cheeks.

"No photos!" Judge Friedman yelled at the journalist. "Court is in recess."

## 24

*Istanbul, Turkey*

MARINA, Cristina, and Eugen planned to meet Petre at the Ciargan Palace Hotel. They were eager to see him, but fearing the kidnappers might still be hiding in the area and surveying them, they decided to meet him in a public park that would be busy with people. They would take a walk in a crowded area toward the Bosphorus River.

"Why did we come to Istanbul?" Petre said, resuming Cristina's questions. "We wanted to follow up on our hunch about Ceausescu's gold. It's easier for us to investigate from Turkey than Iran."

"The premise is that everyone thinks that Sharatt worked for Turkey in this scheme," Eugen stated. "Part of that is true. But his initial calling was to help Iran. Remember, he was born in Tabriz, and his parents still live there. His first citizenship was Iranian, and his first language was Persian."

"His first allegiance went to Khorasami, who was president from 2005-2013," Petre reminded them. "Khorasami was an engineer, specializing in caves, and he developed nuclear sites underground. The sanctions from the U.N. and the U.S. against their nuclear development began during his government."

"Don't forget that our records reveal that Recep's father, Hassan Sharatt, a steel magnate, worked with Khorasami as an economic adviser when the embargo started," Eugen said to his friend. "Sharatt Senior even appeared on the American sanction list and had to pay a hefty fine to the American government. More than $2 million."

"Don't tell me that's how Recep got involved in gold smuggling?" Cristina asked.

"Yes. Like you said, Cristina—fathers and sons. Power sharing."

"Don't forget Rafsanjani, the father of them all," Eugen said. "He was very powerful after 1979, with the downfall of the Shah. But he met his nemesis with Khorasami, who was his political opponent, and had eliminated Rustany as president. Then Khorasami wanted to get rid of Rafsanjani by putting him in jail for corruption. Rafsanjani had to get rid of his gold—Ceausescu's gold—the proof of his corruption."

"Imagine," Marina commented. "This gold smuggling scheme helped Iran avoid international sanctions and then Iran pocketed billions more after they got reimbursed from moneys held in escrow from the same sanctions. It ranks among the largest embargo evasions in modern history!"

"The truth of the matter," Eugen said, turning to his wife and then to Marina, "is that Petre and I have been investigating this case since 2010, because it was related to other crimes in Turkey. We had our first clue when Ozogant was campaigning to become president. We kept getting confidential reports about his bragging that he was adding billions of dollars' worth of gold to the economy as prime minister. We found it suspicious, so we tracked Turkey's export data reports—which strangely, the Turkish government didn't hide—and we saw an unbelievable spike in Turkish gold exports. We couldn't believe the numbers—each day, millions and millions, and we wondered where the Turks were getting it. We both thought of gold from Ceausescu that he had secretly taken personally to Rafsanjani. We went back to our records from Romania that documented Ceausescu had gone to Tehran in December of 1989 with $1 billion worth of gold."

"Eugen and I have a theory," Petre said, "that Ceausescu's billion dollars in gold jump-started the scheme. Rafsanjani used Zanssany, who in turn directed Sharatt and his group on how to get Ceausescu's-Rafsanjani's gold from Iran to Turkey, and recycle the gold back to Iran. Everyone thought the gold came first from Turkey and then to Iran, but no, the opposite. Rafsanjani's billion in gold went to Zanssany, then to Sharatt, who mixed the gold with more gold from Turkey, hid it in the firefighting equipment as part of the humanitarian loophole, and then paid Iran for gas and oil with the gold. Nothing was traceable. Hachebanque, Turkey's national bank, gave phony invoices. And that's how Rafsanjani laundered his gold and washed his hands clean. All before he died so he could go to his Maker purified."

"I always thought that Ceausescu's gold was cursed," Petre said. "Blood gold—stolen from twenty-four million Romanians who were starving and had a miserable life. No one could have more than one light bulb in their entire house, and heat was restricted to one hour in the morning and one hour at night. I remember as a boy, I had to wear my hat and coat at home and in school."

"I also had to wear gloves and a scarf inside my own house, too" Eugen said. "It was miserable."

"We didn't have enough firewood, either." Cristina shook her head, remembering those horrible days. "It was always cold. We were often hungry, and never able to do anything about it."

"Blood gold," Eugen repeated. "It reminds me of Mica's colored diamonds—blood diamonds, she used to call them. They were cursed."

"The downside of so-called treasures," Marina said. "We hunt for them, but we must admit, they have many facets, and aren't always as shiny as they appear."

"Was there another clue that put you and Petre onto the golden money trail?" Cristina asked her husband.

"Yes, it was during the time when Iran was feeling the squeeze from sanctions. I saw a photo in a Turkish newspaper showing Rafsanjani giving an award to a young man, Zanssany: the Top Job Creator award. Zanssany was bowing his head, and his entire body spoke of awe in front of Rafsanjani. Zanssany did become the 'Top Creator,' with Rafsanjani giving him directions like a puppeteer.

"I remember the next week, when the photo was replaced by another photo—Zanssany in jail. Khorasami had realized that Zanssany was working with Rafsanjani—maybe he saw the same photo—and that Zanssany was not sharing the percentage he had promised the government."

"What do you mean?" Marina asked.

"In Iran, the sanctions against selling oil were circumvented through middlemen, who worked as traders in oil for the government. They did the actual financial transactions and received all the earnings. In this way, the government shielded themselves, legally and politically, because they were not doing the deals. Zanssany was the most important middleman. He sold millions of barrels of oil and collected nearly eighteen billion dollars for Iran. However, Iran's Oil Ministry filed a lawsuit against him for not turning over all the money he collected for the government. They claimed he was withholding nearly another three billion. This was much more than his commission allowed. That's why Zanssany was imprisoned and sentenced to death."

"We heard that Sharatt worshipped Zanssany," Cristina commented, remembering Erol's description of the duo. "Sharatt dreamt of being just like his friend—rich, sophisticated, flamboyant. I heard that Zanssany had an aura about him, a charisma, and Sharatt became intoxicated by being around him."

"That's right," Eugen said, nodding his head. "Zanssany organized a group of very well-connected young men in Iran and Turkey and ran his business like the Mafia. He was at the head, directing everyone and everything, but from behind the scenes. Sharatt was his loyal lieutenant. He managed all of Zanssany's finances, even his companies, and deposited a lot of Zanssany's profits into his own bank accounts in Turkey and in his company Safir Altin as a way to protect his idol."

"Oh my God!" Marina shouted. "That confirms why Sharatt left for Miami. The Iranians wanted him to pay up for Zanssany. He was afraid of Iran, not Turkey."

"Did the American government know all this was going on?" Cristina asked.

"Of course. Since 2010, we shared all our findings with the F.B.I., C.I.A., and the Department of State. But they didn't act on it."

"Why not?" Marina asked, surprised.

"They probably didn't want to get the Iranians or the Turks angry. The Americans wanted to use Turkey's air base at Incirlik in southern Turkey against ISIS. They also wanted Iran to sign the treaty of non-proliferation and stop their nuclear activities—Hommett's legacy."

"Yes, all these years, the American government looked away," Petre said, "even let Turkey back Hezbollah, ISIS, and al-Kettaba. And the Americans knew since 2013 about Iran and Turkey using a legal loophole to transfer gold for gas."

"Such a list of wrongs," Petre whispered. "The Americans didn't want Recep's inside information to become public. That's why they gave him immunity. Made a deal, and put him in the Witness Protection Program to silence him.

"The American government knew from the beginning that Hachebanque was the conduit for all these criminal transactions. Hachebanque, bought gold and helped Sharatt transport the gold to Iran. Hachebanque signed his fictitious documents—his over-billing invoices and his circular invoices for the same transactions that allowed him to triple his profits. When business mounted into tens of billions of dollars and gold, Hachebanque got other Turkish banks involved, including eight international banks that were registered in New York City."

Cristina interrupted. "You say Hachebanque. Who was the person in charge and signing the invoices?"

"Mohamet Akan. The man who is being tried now in New York," Eugen answered. "He signed all the invoices as deputy CEO and general manager of Hachebanque. He was Sharatt's banker. How do you think Akan got $50 million to offer for bail in New York?"

"But Sharatt didn't pay Zanssany's bill to the Iranians. He ran away instead. I guess he needed a vacation in Miami," Cristina said.

"The net result," Eugen summarized, "is that we see the Turkish people demonstrating in the streets."

Eugen kicked a stone that was in his way. "There were things that Petre and I knew but were never allowed to talk about. We looked away while Iran and Turkey committed crimes. I feel ashamed of myself."

Cristina put her arm around her husband. "The story isn't over," she said, trying to comfort him. "Akan's trial is going on. Sharatt is a witness for the Americans, and he's scheming now about how to save his skin. There will be more."

Marina nodded her head. "I remember Tahquitz told me a Taoan saying—three things must come out: the sun, moon, and truth."

"I wonder if the reason why we were kidnapped will ever come out?" Cristina said.

"Who knows what's the truth? Politics can be mysterious."

"Yes," Marina agreed. "Politics can offer hope and risk—no different from life—no different from a treasure hunt."

Suddenly, they heard a buzz coming from Petre's backpack.

"What's that?" Marina asked.

"An alert that I set up to remind me when CNN is transmitting the continuation of Akan's trial. It's being live-streamed now."

"Will Recep reappear as a witness?"

"No. Looks like he's hiding. He's officially in the Witness Protection Program. But maybe there's another witness. Let's see."

Petre signaled that they should follow him to a quiet area on the grass that was unoccupied. "No one is near. We can sit here and watch it on my tablet."

They sat down and waited until Petre was ready. And then, they were all fixated on the screen.

## 25

*Continuation of the Trial of Mohamet Akan*
*U.S. District Courthouse, Brooklyn, New York*
*Two days later*

*CNN will now take you directly to the trial of Mohamet Hakan Akan, from Brooklyn, New York.*

*For our international viewers who may not follow all the English of the trial, we have posted English captions below.*

*Akan's trial continues despite protests from Turkey's officials and the president of the Turkish Republic. Judge Robert Friedman of the case has announced that there will be a special witness today, December 11, 2017 —Mr. Sadam Corrmasz. The jury is surprised; they were not briefed beforehand about the matter.*

*The deputy-chief U.S. Attorney of Manhattan, Mr. Sam Michaels, will lead the interrogation.*

*"Your Honor and members of the jury," Michaels began, while referring to the notes that Judge Bremen had handed him in the morning. "The next witness will be called on behalf of the United States Attorney's Office for the Southern District of New York. His testimony will serve to*

*prove Mr. Akan's guilt in this case and that of the bank he represents, Hachebanque."*

Michaels approached the jury. "The prosecution presents Mr. Sadam Corrmasz, a former Turkish police supervisor, who arrested Recep Sharatt in Istanbul on December 17, 2013, with three co-conspirators, who were sons of Turkish ministers at that time."

Mr. Corrmasz, a slight man around thirty years old, took the stand. Next to him was a translator.

"Tell the court, please, about your work as a policeman," Michaels began.

"In 2010, I graduated third in a class of 360 police cadets. I worked hard and rose through the ranks in the Istanbul police force. In 2013, I served as a senior ranking police officer on projects related to public corruption."

"Can you explain what happened the evening of December 17, 2013?"

"There was a plane that was registered to the Turkish-based, ULS Airways. The plane had left Accra, Ghana and was en route to Dubai, but had to make an emergency landing at Istanbul's Atatürk Airport because of fog. The customs official who investigated the cargo found that the paperwork was false. Recep Sharatt, who was the lead member of the crew, had filled out documents stamped by Hachebanque that listed the cargo at 1.2 tons of ordinary metals. But the metals were not ordinary— they were gold. $65 million worth of gold in three thousand pounds of bullion bars. The cargo was registered as belonging to Master Saranson Tourism Company owned by Balal Zanssany and his wife at the time, Soraya Asadi."

"How did you learn that the plane had to make an emergency landing? Who contacted you?"

"The chief of the Turkish Intelligence Agency. They'd had Recep Sharatt on their radar screen since before 2013. They were the first to reveal a variety of schemes involving Sharatt and Hachebanque with Turkish and Chinese joint ventures. All of them created shell companies and used Dubai as the headquarters."

"What did these shell companies do?"

"They transferred currencies into gold and exchanged the gold for Iranian oil."

"What an irony," Park commented. "It was the Turkish Intelligence Agency that picked up the corruption that led to the C.I.A. and F.B.I. to follow up."

Several journalists in the room laughed.

"Why do you think the plane was going to Dubai and not to Tehran?" Michaels continued his interrogation.

"Probably to hide the money in Dubai."

"Objection!" came the voice of the lead defense attorney. "That is an opinion based on speculation."

"Sustained," said the judge.

Michaels changed course. "What happened after you got a call from the intelligence agency?"

"The customs official called my unit about the matter after he reviewed the plane's documents, and found them to be false. I went directly to the airport with my team. We investigated the situation and after several hours, we confiscated the cargo, sealed the plane for illegal paperwork, and arrested Sharatt and his friends who were on the plane with him."

"Did you know Mr. Sharatt before December 17, 2013? Had you heard about him?"

"No, I did not know Mr. Sharatt. Yet several men in my unit had recognized him as having a celebrity wife and seeing pictures of him in magazines with Belcan Ozogant, the son of the prime minister at the time.

"What did you do next?"

"I secretly contacted a prosecutor I knew in Ankara and asked him to investigate the case. Two days later, he got back to me that he had found a money trail that showed Sharatt had paid $63 million dollars in bribes to ministers in the government. He named who they were: Hachebanque's general manager at that time, Hachebanque's deputy C.E.O., Turkey's minister of the economy, the minister of the Interior, minister of War. And Mohamet Akan." He pointed to the well-dressed man in the first row.

"The next day, my team and I secretly searched Sharatt's primary residence and found dozens of shoeboxes filled with stacks of money. There were piles of hundred dollar bills and 500-euro banknotes. I took photos of them that I believe the court has."

"Yes, we have them, Mr. Corrmasz. Did you count all the money?"

"I did. There were 45 million euros in boxes with a label for Mr. Caglan. Then another 100,000 euros labeled for Mr. Gul's son, and more shoeboxes with $200,000 in $100 bills, labeled also for Mr. Gul's son."

"Did you find anything else?"

"Yes, shoeboxes filled with jewelry and another box with a recorded phone call between Ozogant and his son, Belcan. Sharatt must have gotten it somehow and was keeping it in case he needed it for the future. Whatever the reason, it was there, and Belcan's voice was very identifiable. He had told his father that their house was being searched. Father told son to get rid of the cash in the house."

"What did you do with the gold found in Sharatt's plane and money in his house?"

"I deposited it in our police corruption unit's bank. I can't vouch what happened to it after that, but I handed over to your court the official copy of my deposit slip with the date."

"Yes, we have those as well. Please, Mr. Corrmasz, tell us what did you do with the taped conversation you found."

"I kept it—for proof and protection. Then I finally gave it to the F.B.I."

"What happened to your investigative reports?" Michaels asked.

"I made photocopies and gave them to my mother."

"And then what happened?"

"The investigation took a few days. On December 22, 2013, five days after Sharatt and his friends were arrested, all the police in my unit on this case, 200, were fired or reassigned or put in prison."

"And you?"

"I was sent a thousand miles away from Istanbul to protect a bridge in the city of Hakkari, near the Iraqi border."

"Sounds like you were exiled. And kept far away from the press. How long did you stay there?"

"Nine months."

"After that, were you reinstated to your unit in Istanbul?"

"No. I was imprisoned for eighteen months—until February 9, 2016."

"And then?"

"Six months later, in August 2016, I was set free. That's when I escaped from Turkey. It was a hard thing to do because the government had taken away my passport. But I found a smuggler. I paid him with money my mother, brother, and two sisters gave me. I traveled through three countries until a contact introduced me to C.I.A. agent, who put me in touch with the F.B.I."

"Did you escape alone?"

"No, I met up with my wife and daughter, and escaped with them."

"Were you able to make a copy of the entire investigative file?" Michaels asked.

"Not everything. But I did take photos of the piles of gold in the plane with Mr. Sharatt and stacks of money in the shoeboxes. I also handed over to the F.B.I. an encrypted flash drive that contained classified information of emails, letters, wiretapped conversations, banking documents, and photos."

Michaels turned to the judge. "With permission, Your Honor, after Mr. Corrmasz finishes his testimony, can I submit a photo of the gold bars for exhibit number one as evidence, and also play for the jury the tapes we have from Mr. Corrmasz?"

"Yes, but continue first with the witness's testimony."

The lawyer did as told.

"Mr. Corrmasz, what did the F.B.I. and U.S. government do for you in return for your flash drive, tapes, photos, documents, and cooperation?"

"They have put me, my wife and my daughter in a Witness Protection Program and have promised us American citizenship."

"Are you satisfied with this arrangement?"

"Yes, I have freedom, sir. But I left the country that I love. I worry for the safety of my family that I left behind."

"Can you explain?"

"In my investigation and in my report to U.S. officials, I have documented who the number one person guilty in this case is. I know he will learn about my findings and take revenge on me, my mother, brother, and sisters." He paused and looked down. "I fear for them. I'm responsible."

"I understand your concern. I assure you that we will get them to another country safely and under the U.S. Whistleblower Protection Act. We appreciate your courage to come forward."

## 26

*Istanbul, Turkey*

THE FOUR FRIENDS REMAINED QUIET, lost in their own thoughts.

Marina broke the silence. "I would imagine after such a witness, Akan will be found guilty."

"For sure," Cristina agreed. "Especially with tangible proof, such as photos, tapes, documents, and all that Corrmasz has given to the F.B.I."

"Will President Ozogant accept Akan staying in prison in the U.S.?" Petre asked. "Hachebanque is still Turkey's official government bank. It doesn't look good for him. Elections are coming up."

"I would think discussions are going on now behind closed doors," Eugen said. "These kinds of deals can take time."

"It depends on how important Turkey becomes for the Americans in the Middle East."

"In any event, the story's not over," Cristina said.

"My wife is brilliant." Eugen kissed her and they all laughed. "So, my genius, can I offer you a tour of my exotic hotel room?" He winked at her.

"That's our cue, friends," Marina said, smiling. "I have a date with Tahquitz. So, I'll leave you as well for the afternoon. Dinner at 8:00 at your exotic hotel?"

They all kissed cheek-to-cheek, happy that they were together.

*"Ciao ciao,"* they whispered, and they went their own ways.

---

Marina walked towards the spice market where she was to meet Tahquitz. Cristina stayed with Eugen. Petre had joined forces with Istanbul's chief of police to track down the kidnappers, leaving Marina to stroll alone through the city streets. What could be a better reward for her recent day of horrors than to wander through the Grand Bazaar, a labyrinth of treasures?

The Grand Bazaar has been the soul of Istanbul for centuries—known to house more than 4,000 shops, 2,000 studios and 500 stalls in an area of sixty-seven streets that crisscross and interconnect into a labyrinth of alleys. Only Aladdin, with his flying carpet, could find his way. Today, it's very much the same. The only thing missing is an acrobat and a dancing bear.

Marina stared overhead at the mosaic ceiling as she meandered through the covered section. Vendors were shouting their wares in multiple languages. Women with headscarves carried heavy bundles on their shoulders. An elderly man with a red fez stood in front of his stand of round pitas sprinkled with bits of tomato and onion. A young boy strolled the area with a silver samovar strapped to his back, and every few minutes, he'd pour for a customer a brew from flowers and fruit. Marina felt as if she were part of a fairytale.

She continued on, following the fragrance of orchards and sandalwood that mixed with musty goods. Nearby was a vine-shaded courtyard of secondhand books that tempted her to linger a while. There were dozens of translated books from world authors mixed with Holy Korans bound by leather and jewels, and she delighted herself with such treasures.

Soon the flower market, with a sweetness of paradise, lured her on to another section where a group of customers were searching among second-hand clothes with the hope to find a better suit or coat. She paused and looked above her, where dozens of old jackets swayed from ceiling hooks.

Next to them were dozens of dangling cobalt-blue ceramic good luck charms of varying sizes and shapes: Turkish evil eyes, amulets to ward off the evil eye and to protect the wearer from forces of misfortune and curses. Marina smiled; she should have worn at least one before she was kidnapped.

Farther up the hill and beyond the clothes bazaar was a fruit market with carts of pink and white strawberries, piled like pyramids standing guard over the other stacks of red cranberries, blue mulberries, and purple lingonberries. She marveled at the mosaic of colors from Turkey's Ottoman Empire.

She smelled sweetness wafting from dozens of stalls containing rows and rows of *loukoumi*, soft Turkish nougat made from walnuts, chestnuts, figs, lemon, rose petals, or chocolate. At each kiosk, a mustachioed man smiled and tempted her with a square of Turkish delight from his magical display.

Marina continued on, wanting more, as she followed the lane of jewelry stalls of silver and gold that led to copper and brass wares until her passage was blocked by carpets heaped together on the floor in Ali Baba splendor. She stopped at the section of rugs to admire the glory of past times. A merchant and British gentleman were bargaining, and Marina smiled as she eavesdropped. The merchant pulled down a thick, wine-colored rug from its hook, showed it to the customer, and caressed it as if he were in love with its wool. Then he rolled it out in front of the man. "It's from a three-month-old lamb. Feel it. Like the skin of a woman." The merchant laughed, showing broken teeth and a wide smile.

She watched as they continued the charade of arguing. "It's not worth that much," said the British customer. Five times the rug merchant wrinkled his face and stroked the carpet, called it a princess of virgin wool. Five times the customer walked away only to be called back, while he shook his head and rolled his eyes in a cat-and-mouse-game of bargaining. Finally, the Brit agreed on a price and while laughing with pleasure, paid the merchant and smiled. "Please, keep the change."

Marina looked at her watch, realized it was time to leave, and then asked the rug merchant how to get to the spice market.

She saw Tahquitz at the main entrance and waved. He hurried toward her and hugged her. "We'll meet two of my friends who can show you their creams, made from flowers and herbs. We're a little early."

He led her inside toward the entire section of the market devoted to soaps, oils, and lotions. She picked up one soap after another, took deep whiffs, and gave the man a smile as he watched her with his treasures.

"Let me call Avi to reconfirm our meeting," Tahquitz whispered to Marina, holding his phone. "I'll have to go outside for better reception."

"I'll wait for you here," she said and continued her hunt for something unusual.

"Give me a few minutes." Tahquitz left while Marina spoke to the merchant, who was eager to practice his English. Then suddenly Marina put the soap down and took a deeper whiff of the air that was no longer sweet. She closed her eyes to recognize the odor, and then yelled, "Fire! Fire!"

She looked around to see where it was coming from and if it were near. Before she could move, the smell of fire burning wood overwhelmed her. The smell evoked a flashback of Stefan.

When Stefan had arrived in New York after escaping Romania, he looked like he had aged years, he was so thin and weak.

"I'm here. What happened to me is over," he said, kissing her. "I'm still strong enough to love you." He placed her softly on the sofa and whispered, "Before I tell you what happened to me, I want my reward." They laughed and made love through the night.

"Now I have everything," he whispered to her on their pillow. "I love. I am loved. I have so much to look forward to."

He didn't want to tell her exactly what had happened to him in Romania when he was arrested for trying to leave the country. "All I will say is that I suffered. The Communists knew I wanted to escape."

Once Marina and Stefan knew they wanted to spend their life together, they decided to emigrate. It was a hard thing to do—leave their families and country. But Marina was determined to make something of her life with the possibilities that the West could offer. The plan was that she would leave first to West Germany with Mica's help, and then Marina would work with Mica's lawyers for Stefan's release. That's when he was arrested. Someone must have reported to the Authorities that he had submitted papers to emigrate. That was a crime during Communism.

While making love, she had seen burn marks on his back, chest, legs, arms, and bottoms of his feet, but he wouldn't talk about them.

Weeks later, however, he finally told her what had happened to him as he tried to escape.

He was to wait at an abandoned glass factory for a smuggler to lead him to the Romanian-Hungarian border. But the smuggler didn't show up. Stefan waited for the entire night and fell asleep. He was awakened by a fire in the factory. The smuggler had sold Stefan's location to Romania's Secret Police, who had set the fire to trap him inside. Stefan was able to get out at the last minute despite wooden beams crashing down in front of him. Then outside, the police were waiting.

---

Marina smelled fire and ran. She heard a loud crash near her. She ran in the opposite direction from the falling beams. But there were other wooden planks in her way, and then a large burning board fell at her feet. People were screaming and running. Marina tried to jump over the burning wood, but the flames were too high. She screamed for help, but no one stopped.

She tried to follow the other people who were escaping, but another beam fell at her feet. Smoke kept her from seeing where to go. She panicked, not knowing whether she should run to the left or to the right. She couldn't figure out where she was. She yelled for help again, and then like a miracle, she heard her name.

"Marina! Here! Here!" It was Tahquitz. A wooden beam came down between them.

She fell.

---

She awoke and felt the cool air and hard ground. Tahquitz was slapping her on the cheek.

"Marina, speak to me!"

"What happened? she moaned, rubbing smoke from her eyes.

"The firefighters came immediately and put out the fire. It was an accident. It burned down the section where you were."

She stared at him. He was holding her hand.

"You're safe. You haven't been hurt." He kissed her cheeks. "I won't let anything happen to you."

She smiled at him in a strange way.

"What's amusing you?" he asked.

"I really should have bought a Turkish evil eye for protection."

## 27

*Paris, Les Arènes de Lutece*
*June 1, 2018*

"AVANCEZ. START NOW!" came the clear orders from Cristina Patrisse, Paris's leading fashion designer. *"Passez,"* she told each of the twelve models as they marched one by one into Les Arènes de Lutece. It was the first fashion show in Paris that had ever been held in the city's ancient Roman colosseum.

Cristina pressed the button for Mozart's Violin Concerto Number 5, *Turkish,* and the sounds of violins and cellos announced each model's appearance. It was June in Paris, and Cristina was introducing her new collection of Turkish harem pants. Each loose-fitting garment was made from embroidered flowers with fourteen-karat gold stitching that shone brilliantly in the sun. Their bare chests were covered by thin strips of matching fabric.

As the twelve models paraded around the amphitheater, their red fezzes and black tassels swayed with the music. On the side of each hat was a blue Turkish evil eye to ward off misfortune. Cristina's assistant handed the corresponding photo of the designs to journalists as each model passed by.

Marina sat in the middle of Tahquitz, Cemele, Eugen, Mica, André, Anca, and Petre. They were applauding Cristina's creative touch of coordinating the model's color of harem pants with the chic design. Laughing, the friends delighted in the excitement that Cristina's fashions were inspiring in the press. Beauty and art combined with the exotic to reassert Cristina's mark in Paris's fashion world.

A cocktail reception followed and was held in the center arena of the colosseum.

Cristina had coordinated every detail and arranged the buffet table with pink and red roses next to white lilies. She stood at the head of the table and greeted each guest.

When her circle of friends approached from the receiving line, Cristina took the microphone and said, "Silence please. I want to dedicate this fashion show to the people of Turkey, whom I have learned to love, and especially to my dear friends Tahquitz and Cemele, who are my saviors—my heroes. I don't want to go into details now, but I wish to say that without them, my best friend Marina and I would not be here, today. I would like to raise my glass and toast Tahquitz and Cemele. Please join me."

Everyone raised their glasses. The two men stood, but modestly, lowering their heads, embarrassed.

Tahquitz asked Cristina for the microphone and said, "If I may, I would also like to make a toast, to my future wife, Marina, who traveled with Cristina into the hidden underground secrets of Turkey." He raised his glass. "To Marina. Next week, we'll be married in New York."

Cristina, Anca, and Mica hugged Marina and took her hand to dance as the music played Mozart's concerto. The four friends went into the center of the amphitheater, holding hands, and sang, "We are the poets of our lives."

# 28

*New York City, several days later*

RUBBING SLEEP FROM HER EYES, Marina woke up early to the sound of birds outside her Manhattan apartment. She couldn't sleep—she was so excited about the preparations for her wedding. On Friday, she and Tahquitz would be married at a private ceremony at her apartment, followed by a reception.

She ran down the circular staircase and turned the lights on in the kitchen. Looking out her terrace over Central Park, she marveled at how beautiful June was in New York City. It reminded her of mornings in Transylvania when she was a girl, when the fields were covered with flowers. Her mother would prepare tea with honey and toast thick with rose petal jam for her. Marina felt the same way now—happy, but even happier, appreciating the joy that the coming days would bring. She loved Tahquitz. He had given her a feeling of peace that she had never known before, not even as a child.

Marina opened her computer on the marble counter. But

before checking the day's news, she switched to her email. She wanted to send a message to Tahquitz, who was in Santa Fe for another day. She could have phoned him, but it was too early; in the middle of the night for him. She calculated a two-hour time difference. She'd have to wait a day to talk to him in person.

"It's easier for me to put my thoughts down in a letter first and follow up in a couple of hours with a phone call," she said to herself. So she typed.

My Dear Tahquitz,

As I look back at my past and conjure up the cast of people who have played important roles in my life, I realize that a person's willpower is not the only director of one's actions. Willpower, however, is what linked me to Cristina, Mica, and Anca since we were teenagers. We thought we could fight whatever obstacle came our way because of our determination. But life taught us differently. There were other forces, stronger than us, stronger than our will, as fate, nature, health, good and bad luck.

These thoughts came to me a year and a half ago, when I heard that Rafsanjani had died. I was pulled back to Christmas 1989 in Transylvania. It was a horrific time of blood and revolution, when Romanians wanted to get rid of a dictator who for twenty-four years had destroyed their lives. We were suffering while Ceausescu was getting rich. So rich that he had a surplus of $1 billion in gold to hide with Rafsanjani in Tehran. Ceausescu thought he was invincible, and he'd be able to survive the revolution and recoup his fortune in Iran.

I wondered what happened to the gold that Ceausescu stole and hid and was never able to claim.

Fate took me to clues for an answer that began as a treasure hunt in Santa Fe—to you—then to you again on another treasure hunt in Istanbul to get closer to the truth.

But fate took a twist, and good times turned dark. When Cristina and I were kidnapped, I kept thinking of possible tragedies that could befall us. I tried to stay calm and could only do so by thinking of you–hoping that you would come soon to help us. And you did!

It was then that I realized my life would have little meaning if I couldn't share it with you. I wanted so much to live and to love you. I wanted to tell you how dear you are to me. How you'd saved me from a life of selfishness. From a life of not loving.

I wonder—was it my willpower that kept me searching for you all these years? Or was it fate? Or good luck? The greatest reward from my life's search is that I have found you. And that is the most important treasure.

The political case we were all so obsessed with has not finished. Despite the attention several journalists have given the case, even a dedicated Pulitzer Prize recipient in Istanbul, it has not received sufficient coverage in the States. I imagine that the American politicians are not sure what to do with the facts—squash them, spin them or use them for political gain.

We do know that Recep is in the Witness Protection Program. But we don't know where he is or who he's with. Most likely he's bleached his hair and has had plastic surgery. Yet journalists are still searching for him. I read recently that he was spotted in Manhattan, dining in a sushi restaurant. But what information did he and his seventeen lawyers give the Manhattan U.S. Attorney? There must be more hidden in the dirt about Hachebanque that's being mulched and buried by Ozogant and Hoss. (I do feel sorry for Deniz, though—I know she loved him. I heard she filed for divorce. Do you know if she'll be staying in that lovely house?)

We're still not sure of the political players of this case who are lurking in the background, playing marionettes for our

President. Why did Scarpia travel to Ankara to speak to Ozogant?

Will our president claim it's fake news if the truth comes out? Will his cronies be interrogated? Become collateral damage? What about the president of Turkey? Will he keep his family protected as son and son-in-law continue sniveling in the family business? Will Mohamet Akan be released from his Manhattan jail and become the chief of Turkey's Stock Exchange, as Ozogant has promised him?

Iran continues to search for their billions in oil commissions that may be stashed away somewhere in Dubai. Or is it in a treasure chest in Malta? Zanssany is still in Tehran's Evin Prison, scheming how to free himself from crimes against the earth.

Strange how the facts of our story overtook us to the point that we, as characters, merged with reality, when fact and fiction began our treasure hunt in Santa Fe.

Just recently, BBC and CNN announced that the Fenn treasure has been found: "*It was under a canopy of stars in the lush, forested vegetation of the Rocky Mountains and had not moved from the spot where I hid it more than 10 years ago,*" Forrest Fenn wrote in his announcement. "*I do not know the person who found it, but the poem in my book led him to the precise spot... The treasure, estimated to be worth over $1 million, was a way for me to inspire people to explore nature and to give them hope.*"

As I write you this letter and I think of you, I remember the beginning of our story on a treasure hunt. How lucky we are to have found each other. And I've been so happy working with you these past months. It has been exciting to share our interest in plants and search for beauty. But I would like to take a pause in our work, and address a request that just came to my desk.

Yesterday, I received a phone call from a British publisher. His name is William Spencer from Hogartte Press. He said that the British are fascinated by the gas-for-gold laundering scheme.

"They'd be eager to read more about what's related to $1 billion worth of gold," he told me.

Then he asked me, "Would you be interested in writing a book about the case?"

"Why me?"

"You've been recommended to us by Gaby Stern, your former publicist, and now ours. She said you have written scintillating product reviews and could also write a book. In addition, people have read about your being kidnapped and what you have experienced. They're intrigued. Your name would help market the project."

I hesitated.

"We'd like to highlight several of the characters involved," he said. "Perhaps you could show them from all sides–motives, background, heart, mind. We believe you could create a new literary style where real and imaginary characters interact with each other to reveal their motives. Use a modern format of blogs, videos, tweets, live-streaming, and photos with narrative text and factual data. Make it captivating for the young and old."

I wasn't sure, and I told him, "I'm not a writer or journalist. And I'm not British."

He persisted, "You interacted with people who were involved in the case. They confided in you. And, because you're not Turkish or Iranian, you can be more objective. Not take sides. We want the truth."

"Would this be for your non-fiction or fiction division?" I asked.

"We're thinking of mixing the two genres—a hybrid—make

the factual exciting by including elements of fiction. And make the fiction more believable by including facts. Give the story more realism.

"You could be innovative. Perhaps a *nonfiction novel,* in which actual events are woven together with fictitious conversations using storytelling techniques. You could mix elements from other literary genres, as history, drama, satire, mystery, thriller, and romance. Readers love violence and crime, sex, and love. Include a few photos and maps to highlight actual places and true characters. Seeing is believing. Make it visual as well as literary."

"Quite a challenge," I replied. And then I thought out loud: "Perhaps I could use the case to recreate a treasure hunt. The characters can search for what's important to them. Some will have good luck, some bad luck. But they will all use their willpower in their own way to show what's in their heart."

He thought it was a valid premise—a good way to start. Begin with a treasure hunt and end with a nugget of gold.

And now, as I reflect on the project, I would like to know if you would write the book with me. Our treasure hunt. Not for beauty but for something deeper than the skin. Truth and Justice without lies.

My dear Tahquitz, I have the strength to do this because of you. Because I love you.


Just as Marina stopped typing to reread her letter, the phone rang.

"It's me. I wanted to tell you I love you. And because of my love, I want to do what's important—with you."

"I was just typing the same words to you."

"Telepathy. We're on the same wave length. I hear you talking to me as if you're in my arms.

"Marina, my dear, I wanted to tell you that I'm so happy I found you."

# AFTERWORD

Dear Reader,

Since I finished *Treasure Seekers* in September 2020, several journalistic reports have substantiated the political intrigues I described in my novel. It is only *after* I wrote *Treasure Seekers* that the facts emerged publicly about the criminal activities in Turkey and Iran, and America's awareness of them.

I begin my novel with the criminal investigation of Halkbank, a state-owned Turkish bank, accused of funneling billions in gold and cash to Iran while Iran is under international sanctions. The arrest of the facilitator for the scheme—Reza Zarrab—sets up the cause and effect of the novel's structure. From a literary technique, the scandal and arrest allow me to mix fact with fiction—the facts of the multibillion-dollar gas-for-gold laundering scheme, with my fictional characters, Marina and Cristina.

The long-time friends from Transylvanian vacation in Turkey, eager to enjoy Istanbul; that is, until real-life characters pull them into the secrets of a laundering scheme. Unwillingly, the fictional characters become involved with the real political characters, and end in a terrifying hostage situation.

The approach I've used is to merge fact with fiction for a hybrid story that alternates between fantasy and reality. The fiction tells of love and discovery, while the facts reveal how the criminal scheme was accomplished by using courier accomplices, fake documents, a web of international front companies, and loopholes used for sham "humanitarian purposes."

My goal is to reveal the facts of the political scandal by using poetic license in fiction—a deliberate ruse—and a new use of fiction. This hybrid approach encourages readers to travel along with the story and follow the clues as if they were detectives.

The true factual plot reveals how Reza Zarrab, Iranian-Turkish-Azerbaijani-Macedonian citizen along with Mehmet Hakan Atilla, deputy manager of Halkbank, and Babak Zanjani, Iranian billionaire, used their talents to represent their countries and fool the world. And yet, the American government had had their antennas fixed on these rogues since 2013 and even before.

It was not until Reza Zarrab entered Miami's international airport in March 2016 with his rock-star wife and five-year-old daughter, seemingly headed for a family vacation to Disney World, that our government took action. Zarrab was fully aware that he was wanted by the American government for a verdict *in absentia* from 2013 that accused him as the leader of the scheme, along with sons of Turkish officials and Halkbank. As soon as Zarrab entered Miami, he was handcuffed and sent to a Manhattan jail. The lawyers at the Southern District of New York were eager to learn why Zarrab had allowed himself to be arrested.

On October 24, 2019 the United States Senate accused Halkbank of fraud, money laundering, and sanction evasion on Iran. This indictment also listed eight banks involved on behalf of Halkbank: Deutsche Bank, Bank of America, JP Morgan Chase, Citibank, HSBC, Standard Chartered, UBS, and Wells Fargo.

In *Treasure Seekers,* I recreate the actual trial scene of January

2018 in Manhattan accusing Atilla of laundering billions of dollars of gold and cash for Turkey's national bank. The key witness for the American government was Atilla's partner in crime, Zarrab, who quickly testified as to how the largest racket scheme in history was maneuvered by the Turkish president, his ministers and his family.

The questions I address in *Treasure Seekers* are:

- Why did Zarrab want to be arrested and jailed in the United States?
- How was he protecting his best friend Zanjani who had already been incarcerated in Tehran since 2013, for "crimes against the Earth," and for withholding $2.7 billion from the Iranian Ministry of Petroleum for his oil commissions.
- Why did President Trump agree to end further investigations of Turkish officials and Halkbank at the insistence of the Turkish president?

On October 24, 2019 the United States Senate accused Halkbank of fraud, money laundering, and sanction evasion on Iran.

One year later, the U.S. Justice department officially charged Halkbank with criminal activities. The appeal trial, as of now, is scheduled for May 2021 in Manhattan. But unanswered is why not one individual has been charged to the money laundering, bank fraud, or conspiracy to violate U.S. sanctions on Iran.

As of October 30, 2020, with facts emerging from page one of the *New York Times* about these Turkish-Iranian schemes, phony documents, and millions of dollars in bribes, there are still missing details. However, I believe that time will give us some answers to the following omissions:

- How did the laundering scheme help finance Iran's

nuclear program? How many of the facts were known to president Trump and his administration?

- Why was President Trump so eager to please the Turkish president?
- What were the roles of Rudolph Giuliani, Michael Flynn, and Michael Mukasey? Why did they visit Ankara two months after Trump entered office in 2016?
- Why did Reza Zarrab turn witness at the trial of his co-conspirator, Atilla?
- Why was Zarrab placed in the American Witness Protection Program?
- Is there a connection with the gas-for-gold laundering scheme that produced the dismissals of two U.S. Attorneys for the Southern District of New York?

In *Treasure Seekers,* I have tried to answer some of these questions under the guise of poetic license. I join my female characters as we search for justice. The facts of the story cannot be squelched. Political secrets should not be quieted when facts show that a crime is a crime. Even if the details are revealed in a novel.

—Roberta Seret, Ph.D., November 1, 2020, New York City